A
Harlequin
Romance

OTHER
Harlequin Romances
by MARY CUMMINS

1350—ABOVE RUBIES
1404—DIAMONDS ON THE LAKE
1435—SCARLET SUNSET
1482—THE MONKEY PUZZLE
1568—SEA TANGLE
1612—MISTRESS OF ELVAN HALL
1652—A PEARL FOR LOVE

Many of these titles are available at your local bookseller, or through the Harlequin Reader Service.

For a free catalogue listing all available Harlequin Romances, send your name and address to:

HARLEQUIN READER SERVICE,
M.P.O. Box 707, Niagara Falls, N.Y. 14302
Canadian address: Stratford, Ontario, Canada.

or use order coupon at back of book.

A PEARL FOR LOVE

by

MARY CUMMINS

HARLEQUIN BOOKS   TORONTO
WINNIPEG

Original hard cover edition published in 1972
by Mills & Boon Limited, 17 - 19 Foley Street,
London W1A 1DR, England

© Mary Cummins 1972

Harlequin edition published January, 1973

SBN 373-01652-2

•

Printed in Canada

CHAPTER I

Catherine woke suddenly, her heart pounding with fright, as a shaft of sunlight hit her eyes. Then she relaxed as she realised she was in the now familiar bedroom in the Neills' home.

It was a pretty bedroom, tastefully decorated, but Catherine was growing to dislike it, and to feel more and more that she was an interloper in the house, and only there because the Neills were the sort of people who would never ask her to go, however much they wanted the house to themselves again. Would it have been the same if she and Philip had been married? wondered Catherine, and closed her eyes against the sudden pain.

Catherine Lyall . . . Catherine Neill . . . Sometimes she had woken to find herself mumbling the names, and the hot tears had choked in her throat. But after two months it seemed as though her tears were all shed, and her body was healing inside as well as outside. Sometimes, too, she felt the loss of her mother even more deeply than that of Philip.

Soon, she felt, she would have to take up the threads of her life again, and face the fact that she was now alone in the world, with few people on whom she could really depend.

Yet only just over two months ago, she had been a normal, happy girl, looking forward to her marriage, with her mother travelling home from Canada for the wedding.

A quiet wedding had been planned, the guests mainly being Philip's relatives, since Catherine had so few people of her own. Mrs Neill had taken over quite a few of the arrangements, determined that if her son had to marry, then she would do her best to make it a proper wedding. Mrs Lyall had not been well after the death of her husband, and had gone to visit friends in Canada, hoping that the complete change would give her back her full strength and energy.

She had put off her return until the last moment, though she, too, had approved of the marriage, and Catherine had all her preparations made before she received a cable giving the time that Mrs Lyall would arrive at Prestwick Airport.

'We can go down and pick her up in the car, darling,' Philip offered.

Catherine's lovely deep blue eyes showed relief.

'It's a long way to drive from Perth, Philip,' she pointed out.

'Well, if her holiday in Canada has done her a lot of good, we must keep up the good work,' Philip said cheerfully.

They had driven to Prestwick in a happy mood. Mrs Neill had insisted that Mrs Lyall should stay with her for a day or two, instead of going home to the flat she shared with Catherine. Their old home had been sold after David Lyall died, and the new flat was small in comparison, though quite big enough for two.

It had been exciting to meet her mother off the plane, and Philip strapped her carefully into the front passenger seat, while Catherine sat in the back, occasionally leaning forward to speak to both of them.

They had been nearing Perth when the accident happened. Philip had rounded a corner and met two vehicles side by side. Later they said it was a miracle that Catherine had escaped with a few cuts and bruises, though no one could see the long deep wounds inside at the loss of the two people she had loved most.

Catherine had been showered with sympathy because of her double loss, but it was the Neills, and especially Mrs Neill, who had received most admiration. Philip had been her only son, yet she had hidden her grief, and had insisted on nursing Catherine back to health.

But now the girl felt that she had accepted enough, as she dressed to face yet another day, automatically going through the motions of putting on light make-up, and combing out her long dark hair. Mrs Neill needed time, now, to think about herself. She might have come to love Catherine as a daughter in time, but at the moment she was still a young girl, no different from any young girl of her age, living in the Neills' home.

She would go back to the flat, thought Catherine,

as she descended the stairs. She would get a job of some kind, so long as it wasn't in Mr Neill's office of chartered surveyors and estate agents.

'A letter for you, Kate dear,' said Mrs Neill, when Catherine appeared at the kitchen door. 'I went round to the flat and found a small bundle of circulars and, of course, your letter. I wish some of these people who go round pushing circulars through letter boxes wouldn't do it if the house is empty. Seeing them sticking out of the letter box is a complete give-away.'

'How would they know?'

'What, dear?'

'That the house is empty. No, I'll just have coffee, thanks, Mrs Neill.'

'You must eat, Kate. No sense in getting yourself run down.'

What about her? wondered Catherine, looking with a sudden aching heart at the older woman's thin body and pale face. She had never felt closer to feeling love and compassion for this woman.

'Don't worry about me,' she said gently.

'You should give up the flat and move in here with us,' Mrs Neill advised. 'After all, you were within a week of being our daughter.'

'That week made all the difference,' Catherine reminded her, then her voice softened. 'You don't really want me here. You only think you do, and please believe that I appreciate it very much. But we must both now face the fact that we haven't got

8

Philip in our lives. He would have been a link between us and we would have grown to love each other for his sake, but I feel now that we must each go our separate ways. I . . . I want to go back to the flat, and get a job, and . . . well, be independent again.'

Mrs Neill was gazing at the girl, wide-eyed.

' You can't live in the flat on your own, a young girl like you. I . . . I thought we'd done all we could here. . . .'

Catherine bit her lip. It was going to be difficult to make Mrs Neill understand. In fact, she doubted if she could even try. Whatever she said, Mrs Neill would only think her ungrateful, and might even make her *feel* ungrateful.

' I'm sorry,' she said humbly. ' I can't tell you how I feel, but I believe I'm right. You and Mr Neill have been wonderful to me, but I could never take . . . Philip's place . . . in your lives.'

Mrs Neill rose quietly and walked out of the kitchen, and Catherine could hear her going slowly upstairs. She turned to the small bundle of circulars, and the letter in front of her, and turned it over before opening the thick, expensive envelope, then her eyes cleared when she saw that it was signed by Lucille Sheridan. The wedding gift which she had received from the Sheridans had been a beautiful carriage clock. It had been accompanied by a small dainty note of congratulations. Mrs Neill had returned the gifts, and now Lucille was no doubt

9

expressing sympathy. She had been her mother's best friend, and her godmother, but that responsibility had rather slid over the years, except for a pretty pendant for her twenty-first birthday, and the clock as a wedding gift.

Lucille had married James Sheridan, and Alison Lyall had been her bridesmaid. Their son, John, was four years older than Catherine, and Elizabeth was nearer her own age. Catherine knew that the families had rather lost contact with one another over the years, except for a card at Christmas. Yet the Sheridans had often fascinated her, and secretly she would like to have known them a little better.

'They became very successful,' Alison told her daughter, rather ruefully.

'Aren't we successful?' Catherine asked innocently.

'Fishing for freshwater pearls may sound exciting, and can be very successful,' Alison told her, 'but I suppose your father is more successful in that he loves what he is doing and is happy doing it, but financially it hasn't been particularly rewarding.'

'Oh.'

Catherine hadn't really understood till her father died, and their home had to be sold to give them a small income. Now she realised that the large jewellery firm of Sheridan and Rodgers, whose beautiful shop was one of the most attractive in Newcastle, was a far cry from Mrs Lyall and her only daughter, earning a tiny income from making small pieces of fashion jewellery at home.

Catherine pursed her lips as she drew out her letter, and began to read. What could Mrs Sheridan have to say to her, since condolences, she now remembered, had already been sent?

Carefully Catherine read the few preliminaries, then she was reading her letter rather more slowly.

'I know that you won't have anyone left of your own, my dear,' wrote Mrs Sheridan, ' because I remember from our schooldays that Alison only had her parents, who are now both dead, and that David, your father, was already on his own when they married.

' It's sad for a young girl like you to have no one, so we would like you to come to us. John and Elizabeth both work in the shop with James, and if you would like a job, there's always plenty to do there. On the other hand, Balgower is a big house, and although Mrs Bannon is a treasure, we would welcome another pair of hands.

' If you would like to come, James hopes to be in Edinburgh on the sixteenth, and he could come on to Perth and pick you up. If you are still unable to travel, we can make alternative arrangements at a later date. James saw your father just before his death, and he feels David would wish him to sort out any worries you may have, business or private. He can attend to the letting of your flat, and the storage of your furniture, such as you wish to keep. . . .'

Catherine read on, sometimes going back to read parts of the letter twice over. It was a generous offer, kindly made, and her godmother sounded as though she was very considerate. Yet wouldn't she be giving up her freedom if she went to live with the Sheridans? wondered Catherine, then felt a strong distaste for herself. Was she beginning to be suspicious of everyone? Mrs Neill had been kindness itself to her, yet she felt unable to repay her with genuine love. It was as though the accident had robbed her of all feelings.

Now here was her godmother also offering her a home, and a place in family life, and all she could think of was this odd feeling of being absorbed into something against her will.

What was the alternative? wondered Catherine tiredly. She could get a job and stay on with the Neills for a few more months, being accepted because of Philip, or she could go home to the flat, and struggle to pay the bills, living an independent life but paying for her independence with loneliness.

Catherine leaned her elbows on the kitchen table and rested her chin in her hands. The letter was rather a surprise because she had felt that the Sheridans wouldn't want to be bothered with her. Apparently this was quite untrue.

She looked round with a small start as Mrs Neill again came quietly into the kitchen, and Catherine saw that she had been crying, and again felt she hated herself for causing her pain.

'I've had a letter,' she said hurriedly. 'Here, Mrs Neill, you'd better read it. Shall I make more coffee while you do?'

'Please, dear.'

Again there was silence in the kitchen while Catherine boiled up more coffee and Mrs Neill put on her reading spectacles with the blue and silver frames, and slowly read every word.

'Well?' asked Catherine, when she had finished.

'Only you can decide,' the older woman told her. 'But you can say what you think,' urged Catherine.

Mrs Neill faced her squarely.

'Perhaps you are more honest than I am. I wanted you here because you were Philip's choice —all right, I admit it. But maybe you are the one to see most clearly that it wouldn't be good for either of us if we kept you here too long.'

She was silent for a while, and Catherine was breathing a soft sigh of relief.

'Yet . . .' Mrs Neill again looked at the letter. 'Don't let yourself be used, my dear. If the Sheridans give you a home, then you must be grateful to them, but don't go on paying all the time. Remember that you have a lot to give, too.'

Catherine poured the coffee and sat down at the kitchen table again.

'Then you think I shouldn't go?'

'No, but I think you should see Mr Sheridan, and talk to him a little. Sometimes one can learn a lot just by talking to people. Perhaps you could just go on a visit first of all, and come back here if . . . if you don't like the set-up.'

Catherine felt closer to Philip's mother than she had ever done.

' I used to wonder if we'd really get on, you and I, after I married Philip. Now I know we would.'

Mrs Neill nodded. She'd had to get used to Kate's plain speaking, but she had always known how she stood with the girl.

Would the same frank honesty be appreciated by the Sheridans? she wondered, with the hint of a smile. Apparently they had not seen Catherine since she was a schoolgirl, and Mrs Neill again wondered if they realised that she had grown into a beauty. She knew that Philip had been entranced by Catherine's beauty, and one of her greatest attractions lay in the fact that she seemed unaware of how lovely she actually was. Perhaps it would raise further problems the Sheridans had obviously not considered.

' I'll write and say that we'll be pleased to see Uncle James . . .' she broke off, smiling a little. ' At least, I used to call him Uncle James.'

' Yes, do that. Ask him to have tea with us.'

' All right, and . . . thank you.'

' Let's wash up,' said Mrs Neill briskly. ' I don't know where the morning has gone.'

CHAPTER II

Catherine remembered James Sheridan as a tall, rather florid man, with neatly cut dark hair and a small moustache. Now he seemed shorter than she had imagined, his hair now almost white and the small moustache also white. His pale blue eyes looked tired, but his smile was warmly welcoming, when Mrs Neill brought him into the sitting-room where Catherine was resting.

Already she knew that unless she felt, on meeting him again, that living with the Sheridans would be absolutely impossible, she would be going back with him to Newcastle. So after a quick, searching glance, Catherine ran forward to welcome him with a warm hug.

' It's good to see you again, my dear,' he told her, rather huskily. ' You're very like Alison.'

Catherine nodded, but made no comment. The loss of her mother had gone very deep, and she still could not talk about it.

Mrs Neill had gone to fetch the tea tray from the kitchen, leaving them to talk, but Catherine drew her into the conversation immediately on her return. Now that she was leaving, she was also appreciating so much more their kindness to her, and over the past few days she had come to love the woman who might have been her mother-in-law. Sometimes she now had moments of panic when she felt she didn't want to leave the shelter of the Neills' home, but common sense would tell her that this was just reaction to the tragedy of the past two months, and if she was ever to live a full rich life again, she must go and meet its challenge.

' It's very kind of you and Aunt Lucille to have me,' she said with sincerity, and James Sheridan cleared his throat and waved his hand.

' Not at all. You'll be most welcome at Balgower, Kate, believe me. Most welcome.'

Mrs Neill glanced at Catherine as she leaned forward and offered Mr Sheridan the cup of delicate China tea which he'd asked for.

' Mrs Sheridan did say in her letter that Catherine could either have a job in your business, or help with running your home,' she said, then smiled a little. ' Please don't think I'm interfering, but . . . well, Catherine might have been my daughter.'

' Of course. Feel free to set your mind at rest about anything.'

' I just feel that it might be better for her to be sure of some sort of future career, rather than homemaking.'

Mrs Sheridan nodded and turned to the girl.

' Has this been worrying you, my dear? Because it can be resolved quite easily. As you know, Sheridan and Rodgers is a big shop, as jewellers go, with good sales for clocks and watches, as well as jewellery, gold, silverware and precious ornaments.

And I thought you might be interested since your father was such a keen pearl fisherman.'

' I am,' Catherine assured him. ' I got to know the marvellous shop in Perth which specialises in freshwater pearls so well when Daddy was alive. The pearls were made into beautiful brooches and other pieces of jewellery, and I've even been allowed to look at the famous Abernethy pearl. I . . . I've never forgotten it. It was so lovely, and so perfect. One couldn't describe it, really.'

' I know. I've seen it, too,' said James Sheridan, rather ruefully. ' But I'm afraid we only have cultured pearls, and good quality simulated to entice you to Sheridan and Rodgers. Though I think you will find some of the new jewellery designs pleasing. My son, John . . . you remember John? . . . is in charge of jewellery and diamonds, along with myself. Elizabeth looks after the better quality gem stones, necklaces and earrings and small gold charms. My late partner's son, Michael Rodgers, prefers to be with clocks and watches, though everyone can take over from everyone else should the occasion arise.

' Apart from that, we only have Miss Pryce, who has been with us for over thirty years, and who works with Elizabeth, or . . .' James smiled a little, '. . . perhaps I ought to put that the other way round! At one time we also had two more young men, but greater overheads and higher salaries have forced us to cut down a little, so that when Tom

Dearham went off to be manager in a smaller firm, I just couldn't replace him. So . . .' he smiled again . . . ' you'll be most welcome, Kate. I can't imagine that David Lyall's daughter will require much training in jewellery, either. He was always very keen on all forms of gemmology, and became a Fellow of the Gemmological Association for the love of it.'

' Yes, he did,' Catherine nodded. ' I remember watching Daddy when he tested a stone for refractive index, and how he used to know the specific gravity of every stone and its comparative hardness to the diamond. I could practically recite a few of those facts myself!'

' Then you must keep up the good work,' James assured her. ' John and Michael took their F.G.A. examinations a few years ago, and Elizabeth passed hers last year. It shouldn't take you long to study everything you need, and we'll help you all we can.'

He turned to Mrs Neill.

' Does that make you feel any happier?'

Mrs Neill hesitated, feeling that she could hardly discuss financial arrangements. That would be going much too far in her desire to see Catherine well settled and protected. She had no reason to suppose that the girl might be exploited. In fact, they should all be grateful for this opportunity which had arisen. Mrs Sheridan was going to attend to the lease of her flat, and the storage of furniture she wished to keep, while selling off any extra. Catherine would have a small nest egg, enough to make her feel secure should an emergency arise.

'I can see that Catherine will be in good hands, Mr Sheridan,' Mrs Neill smiled. 'I'm very relieved.'

'She has also a fairly long drive ahead of her,' he said, glancing at his watch. 'Are you well enough to travel, my dear?'

'The doctor says it will be quite all right by car,' Catherine assured him. 'I'm only taking a small amount of luggage, though I hope I can send for the rest of my things when I'm settled.'

'I shall keep them for as long as you like,' Mrs Neill assured her, and Catherine felt the sudden rush of tears pricking her throat.

'I can collect them when I come to see about your flat,' James Sheridan suggested. 'You've sorted our personal things, Catherine?'

'Yes.' She turned to Mrs Neill. 'I'll come back and see you soon.'

'Keep in touch,' Mrs Neill urged her, as they parted. 'If you aren't happy . . .'

'I know. I said goodbye to Mr Neill this morning, but my love to him . . . and you.'

Soon she was speeding south in the large comfortable car, and crossing the lovely Forth Bridge.

'We'll rest in Edinburgh for a cup of tea,' Mr Sheridan decided. 'Easy stages will be best.'

It was dark and rather late by the time they drove into Newcastle-upon-Tyne, a city which was strange to Catherine, but even in the dark she was conscious that it was large and interesting, and that the outskirts where Uncle James lived were fresh and lovely.

'You'll have to get to know Northumberland,' he told her, as they drove along quiet roads lined with gently swaying trees which looked ghostly and rather mysterious in the bright moonlight. 'It's a beautiful county, with a great deal of historic interest. John and Elizabeth will be happy to take you sightseeing, I'm sure.'

John and Elizabeth! Catherine felt her heart suddenly quaking a little. She was sure that Uncle James and Aunt Lucille would be happy to have her live with them, but it was only now that she was beginning to realise that she would be in close contact with young people of her own age. Suppose they didn't like her. Suppose they resented her presence in the house.

It was too late to have regrets, however, as the car turned in a gravelled drive between lovely wrought-iron gates, and Balgower, a large imposing house of red brick, with huge bay windows, came into view.

'Here we are,' said Uncle James cheerfully. 'Welcome home, Catherine. Come in, my dear, and say hello to Aunt Lucille and the family.'

There was only Aunt Lucille at home. After Mrs Neill's rather reserved nature, and her quiet but kindly attitude towards her, Catherine found Lucille Sheridan effusive in her welcome. Yet surely that was in her favour. She rushed forward to envelop the girl in a warm hug, her body softly plump, reminding Catherine of a small shapely pigeon.

'Catherine! My dear, you're grown up. And how like your mother. . . . Oh!'

Catherine's smile was a trifle unsteady.

'It's all right, Aunt Lucille. I . . . I've come to terms with what happened. Don't hesitate to talk about Mother . . . or Philip.'

'You poor child!' Lucille's voice was full of sympathy, and she led Catherine into a large spacious lounge, richly carpeted, with deep sofas and armchairs, and long velvet curtains pulled across the windows.

'What a lovely room,' Catherine said sincerely, and knew she had pleased Lucille, who beamed on her, and turned to James, who said he would go straight upstairs to wash and change.

'I'll take Catherine up to her room. Would you like to have a hot drink up in bed, my dear, or would you prefer to come downstairs again for a short while? John and Elizabeth should be in soon, but you can meet them both tomorrow, if you'd prefer that.'

'No, I'll come back down,' offered Catherine.

'She's been ill,' James pointed out, 'and she's had a long journey. She ought to go to bed now.'

'Mrs Bannon has everything ready for you, my dear, and you can have whatever drink you like.'

Suddenly Catherine did feel tired, her body heavy and her head beginning to ache a little.

'All right,' she nodded. 'I . . .'

'Ah, here are the children now,' cried Aunt Lucille, opening the door. 'You're just in time to say hello to Catherine. She's going to bed after her journey.'

Catherine looked curiously at Elizabeth Sheridan as she walked towards her. She was a tall girl, very thin and smart, with sharp features and smoothly coiled reddish-brown hair. She might have been plain but for her superb dress sense. Catherine's eyes were full of admiration, thinking she had rarely seen anyone more striking.

'How do you do,' she said, rather shyly, and found herself being weighed up dispassionately, as Elizabeth shook hands firmly.

'How do you do, Catherine. I hope you had a good journey.'

There was no real warmth in the welcome, but no animosity either. It was as though Elizabeth preferred to reserve judgement as to whether she really wanted to welcome Catherine or not.

Then John Sheridan strode forward, a tall loose-limbed young man with his sister's piercing dark eyes, but a warm, rather lop-sided grin.

'Hello, Catherine,' he greeted her. 'Welcome to the fold. You're a brave lass, taking us on.'

'Oh, John! I'm sure Catherine is most grateful . . . glad, I mean. . . .'

'Grateful,' repeated John. 'Don't forget to be grateful, Kate. It's expected of you.'

'Stop teasing, John,' said Elizabeth. 'You'll have the poor girl all confused!'

Lucille's cheeks were growing slightly pink, but John was laughing as his father walked back downstairs.

'You shouldn't rise to the bait, darling,' he grinned, and James frowned.

'Catherine is too fatigued for your jokes tonight, John,' he admonished. 'Here's Mrs Bannon. She's got everything ready for you, my dear.'

'A warm bath, then bed,' fussed Lucille.

'This way, Miss Catherine,' said Mrs Bannon, a hint of Irish in her accent.

'Goodnight,' she said, a trifle awkwardly, following the stout, grey-haired woman.

'Goodnight!'

'You are a fool, John. . . .'

Catherine could hear Elizabeth's clear voice as she mounted the stairs. He'd told her not to forget to be grateful. Did that mean that she was going to be asked to pay for her new home and family? That, in fact, she was going to be an underpaid assistant?

It really didn't matter, thought Catherine, when she saw her pretty bedroom, decorated in soft shades of lavender. It was the prettiest bedroom she had ever had, and she was glad it wasn't pink. She had never cared for a pink bedroom.

'It's lovely,' she said to Mrs Bannon.

'Indeed it is,' the housekeeper beamed. 'I'm

sure we all hope you'll be happy here, my dear.'

' I couldn't ask for a warmer welcome,' the girl said. There was no need to summon up gratitude. It was all there of its own accord. ' Everyone has been so kind.'

But although her bed was soft as thistledown, and she felt warm and comfortable, sleep eluded her for many hours. She thought about the Sheridans, who were all now so close to her. Uncle James, who looked tired and worried when he was off guard; Aunt Lucille who was warm and soft as a small cat . . . cat? wondered Catherine. Didn't she mean pigeon?

Then there was the smart, attractive Elizabeth, whose looks were so striking, and John Sheridan, with his teasing smile and his ready tongue. Somehow he was not the brisk and smartly competent young business man she had pictured when Uncle James told her he shared responsibility for the diamond jewellery in the shop. She couldn't think of John as an expert on diamonds. Yet a young man, responsible for a large stock of diamonds, would certainly not be a fool!

It was agreed that Catherine should stay at Balgower for two weeks, then start work at the shop in Newcastle, helping Miss Pryce with the cultured pearls. She looked forward to that, but knew the wisdom of resting for a further fortnight, as she still felt shaky, and tired easily.

conditioner for your type of hair.

There's blue for normal hair, pink for dry, green for oily. All rich-lathering. All safe for color-treated hair.

And in a shatterproof bottle, too.

If you've ever said "I just washed my hair and I can't do a thing with it" (and what woman hasn't?) Twice as Nice is the shampoo for you.

Lever Brothers thinks Twice as Nice is so nice, we'll give you 10c just to try it.

Shampoo . . . .

Conditions your hair
while you Shampoo!

The results are fabulous!

← Valuable Coupon

for normal hair
twice as nice®
shampoo & conditioner in one

for dry hair
twice as nice®
shampoo & conditioner in one

for oily hair
twice as nice®
shampoo & conditioner in one

It was a strange sort of fortnight, when she should have got to know her new family rather well, but somehow that didn't happen. She learned that Aunt Lucille led a busy, social life and seemed to be rushing off to various committee meetings.

Uncle James and John both seemed to work long hours, and Elizabeth kept rushing home to dress, and disappear again in her small white Mini, which she drove with little regard to her own safety, or to that of other road users.

' She knocked down the garage doors the day she passed her test,' John informed Catherine solemnly.

' It was your fault. You shut them after I had opened them, and I had no time . . .'

' To notice before flying in,' he agreed.

He often teased his sister, and she railed back at him, but Catherine was aware of a strong bond between them, and sometimes an odd sort of reserve, too, as though there were some things on which they had agreed to differ.

Elizabeth wore a beautiful solitaire diamond engagement ring, and was going to marry Michael Rodgers, whose father had started the business with Uncle James. Michael was at present in London, viewing some new designs in clocks and watches.

' He was ill when the Fair was on at Earl's Court last September,' John informed Catherine. ' He took some sort of 'flu bug, and he was disappointed. He wanted to see the new designs which were available, so now that we're having a fairly quiet spell

25

before Easter, Michael has gone to Birmingham, and on to London for a look-see.'

' I see,' said Catherine. ' Is . . . is his father dead now?'

' Yes.' John's voice was rather brusque, and Catherine wondered if that was because of her own recent loss. ' His father is dead and his mother married again. He lives on his own in a small flat above a shop.'

' Like me,' thought Catherine, feeling a strange affinity with the absent Michael Rodgers. They were both now beholden to the Sheridans for their livelihood, and their emotional needs.

' So he'll be some sort of junior partner?' she asked.

This time John was definitely cagey.

' As I told you, he's in charge of our watches and clocks,' he said flatly, and Catherine felt snubbed. She had no wish to pry further into the running of the firm than was necessary.

' Elizabeth will be happy to see him back again,' she said, rather wistfully, thinking of the times when Philip had been away. And the times when he had returned.

' I guess so.'

Again John's voice was offhand, and Catherine rose. She really did not want to discuss family affairs, so there was no need for him to be so offputting.

' I think I'll go for a walk,' she announced.

' Want me to come? '

' No, thank you. '

Suddenly John was grinning.

' Don't be so stand-offish. Just let me get into my old duds and walking boots. You'd better change those shoes, too, and I'll take you tramping across the fields. We'll let the good Northumberland air blow on those pale cheeks of yours, and the roses will all bloom again. Oh, and I'll ask Banny for some sandwiches. '

Catherine hesitated for a moment. He was an odd and unpredictable young man, she thought. Sometimes he was so deep in thought and so seemingly competent, she felt almost afraid of him. Then he resembled nothing so much as a harum-scarum schoolboy, as he did shortly afterwards when he appeared in old jeans, an anorak, woolly cap and boots, his teeth already biting into an apple, a second one held out to Catherine.

' That's to save you nibbling the sandwiches before we've gone a quarter of a mile. '

Catherine, too, had changed into black slacks and a scarlet anorak, her dark hair caught in a bow at the back, her vivid blue eyes suddenly sparkling.

' I'm not hungry. Oh . . . oh well . . . '

' Come on. Down to the vegetable garden and through the orchard. We'll climb over the fence, then no one will see us eating our apples . . . if that's what you're afraid of. And take off that hair bow. Let your hair down a little. You're so stiff and formal with us.'

Stiff and formal? When she got snubbed if she as much as said the wrong thing?

It was no use arguing, she thought, shaking her long hair free, and feeling the wind blowing it round her cheeks. It really was exhilarating, she thought, as John caught her hand and they clambered over marshy ground, stopping occasionally to look at vast sweeps of landscape, which was already holding great charm for her.

'It looks . . . timeless,' she said.

'Ever seen the Roman Wall?'

She shook her head.

'I'll take you over to Housesteads next Sunday. You'll see some marvellous old Roman ruins, and we can have a look at such places as Hexham, a lovely old town, not so far away.'

'Oh, but won't you . . . ?' She stopped. She had been about to ask if he had no girl-friend to whom he was committed, then remembered that she risked another snub. 'Be busy?' she finished lamely.

He grinned at her again, as though he were infuriatingly reading her mind.

'Of course I will. I'll be busy with you, won't I?'

Then his eyes grew serious.

'How do you really feel about coming here, Kate?' he asked abruptly. 'Did you *want* to come, or was it the lesser of two evils?'

She felt taken aback.

' Of course I wanted to come!'

He was silent as he led her over to a flat stone dyke, where he began to open up their haversack.

' And you had nothing better in mind? Better for yourself, I mean.'

' I hardly had much choice,' she said dryly. ' I'm untrained for a career, and my bank balance isn't exactly enormous. The only thing I know about at all is gem stones, thanks to Daddy.'

John was looking at her curiously.

' But you have assets, or one asset which is worth having.'

' Such as?'

Again his eyes were searching, then they dissolved into laughter.

' More than one, maybe. You're very beautiful, Catherine. That's why . . . I feel reservations about your coming here. I wonder if it was wise, for you, for all of us.'

Her brows wrinkled.

' That can soon be remedied,' she said stiffly, ' if your parents feel the same way . . .'

' They don't, and don't go flying off the handle. Believe me, I'm thinking about you, and your future happiness, my dear.'

There was no doubting his sincerity.

' You speak in riddles, John,' she told him, rather tiredly, and he was immediately contrite.

' Box my thick ear, Kate,' he told her, re-packing

the haversack. 'I'm a clumsy fool. I've brought you too far, and tired you out.'

'No, I'm not really tired. At least, my body isn't. A walk like this should do me good.'

John took her hand as they made their way home rather more slowly.

'Forget all my nonsense,' he told her. 'We all of us have problems, some more than most. Only I'll be looking out for you, Kate. Remember that.'

She felt strangely warmed as she went upstairs again to change. Had she found a real friend in John Sheridan? Yet ought she to take him seriously? And what did he mean by wondering if she had done the right thing coming here? Who could spoil her happiness? Or, come to that, whose happiness could she spoil?

In spite of herself, Catherine shivered a little, and put on an extra sweater. Sometimes it wasn't always so cosy at Balgower.

Catherine asked John to postpone her outing to Housesteads until a later date when Elizabeth came home with the news that Miss Pryce had to go home, feeling ill.

'She had a tooth removed and it's become infected, poor old girl,' she told her mother. 'Her jaw is badly swollen and she feels really off colour, so she must stay at home till she's better.

'Poor woman,' sympathised Lucille. 'You'll be missing her, Elizabeth.'

'Yes. That's why . . . where's Catherine?'

'Helping with some special sort of sweet for dinner. She's good at that sort of thing.'

'Well, I hope she'll be good at selling pearls, because I'm wondering if she's well enough to cope. Getting reasonably good staff is difficult at the moment.'

Catherine was only too happy to oblige. After a week at Balgower, she felt quite rested enough to want to spread her wings a little. There wasn't enough challenge in this well-planned house, which already ran on oiled wheels, to keep her busy all day, and she felt lonely when the family were out at business all day. When Aunt Lucille was at home, Catherine felt, rather guiltily, that the older woman was inclined to get on her nerves. Perhaps they got on each other's nerves, she thought, trying to be fair.

'Are you sure you're fit enough?' Elizabeth asked bluntly. 'Even a large spacious shop like ours can be very tiring, and some customers are infuriating. One must keep one's temper. They spend hours choosing something, then a month or so later they bring it back and ask to swap it for something else. I often wonder if they do the same thing with their furnishings, or clothes, and what reception they get if they do!'

Catherine wondered what reception they got from Elizabeth! She had begun to admire the other girl, even if she never felt close to her. There was no merging of their minds, and sometimes Catherine felt

that the other girl was still viewing her dispassionately, that she kept standing back and having a good
look at her, as though making up her mind about
something. She did not feel wholly comfortable with
Elizabeth.

'I'm fit enough, and I'll rest all I can during my
off-time. Will my plain dress do?' she asked. 'I
suppose I ought to get a few more dresses suitable for
business.'

'It will be fine,' Elizabeth assured her, rather
absently. Her eye ran over the other girl half
enviously. There was no doubt that Catherine was
a beauty, even if she still hadn't learned to make the
best of herself. If she did something about her hair,
and bought clothes which suited her better, she would
be really stunning. Yet perhaps she would lose her
own peculiar look of innocence and freshness, which
could even be her greatest asset. Elizabeth sighed,
thinking how hard she herself had to work to achieve
her own smart appearance.

She thought of Michael, who would be home in two
days' time, and again her eyes swept over Catherine.
How would Michael react to her? For a moment
there was a bleak look in Elizabeth's dark eyes, then
it was gone. There was no use in crossing bridges.
She knew Michael pretty well . . . perhaps better
than he realised. He always knew what was best for
himself.

'Your dark blue dress will be perfect,' she said to
Catherine, in a gentler tone. 'You'll have to be up

early in the morning, so have an early night. I'll take you with me in the Mini. Where's John?'

'Not home yet,' said Lucille.

'Well, we know where he *won't* be,' said Elizabeth dryly, and there was sudden silence which made Catherine look at them both curiously. Where wouldn't John be?

Catherine had already been shown round the lovely jeweller's shop in the busy city centre, but somehow it seemed different in the early morning, viewed from the other side of the counter.

And even that was only a figure of speech. The old counters had now been replaced with lovely glass showcases, attractively displayed, besides which were placed comfortable chairs. Sheridan and Rodgers liked to encourage their customers to take their time, and to enjoy buying something which was meant to give pleasure for many years to come.

Uncle James and John spent some time taking the most valuable displays of diamonds out of the safes, and putting them into the window. Strict rules had long ago been laid down for security reasons, and were kept well up to date, as well as being rigidly followed.

It was Elizabeth who showed Catherine the lovely cultured pearl displays, and the costing of each one so that she was unlikely to make a mistake.

'Always check with me, if you aren't sure,' she advised.

'They're gorgeous,' said Catherine, looking at the milky white pearls, the more expensive ones having diamond clips, sometimes with other precious stones. 'But I wish you could see the freshwater pearls in Perth, Elizabeth.'

The other girl's interest was caught.

'Yes, I'd love to see those. Some time I must go and see them for myself.'

'They're fished out of the Scottish rivers, as you know. Daddy used to do that, of course.'

'Yes, I know,' said Elizabeth abruptly.

'The colours are so unusual, some even pink and mauve besides cream, and the brooch designs are quite perfect, because they're made up with backgrounds of bracken and heather . . . in gold, of course . . . and floral arrangements like snowdrops and bluebells. The biggest of all is the Abernethy pearl, about half an inch in diameter, I believe. I saw it once. It was really beautiful.'

'But . . .'

Elizabeth was looking at her curiously.

'Did you see some of the pearls your father found?'

'Oh yes, but they were usually fairly small, but quite valuable. Nothing exciting, though.'

Uncle James and John came over to speak to her as Mrs Neal, the cleaning woman, was hurriedly giving a final polish to the showcases.

'Put the kettle on, Mrs Neal,' said Uncle James, and she grinned. He was well known for needing a cup of tea long before the usual 'elevenses'.

'Yes, sir,' she assured him.

'Well, Catherine, my dear, are you quite happy? Not worried about anything?'

'Not yet!' she laughed. 'It all seems quite straightforward.'

'You can soon learn all you need to know for the moment, then we'll gradually teach you more. You're also going to learn about people, my dear. In a jeweller's like this, one starts to learn about people very quickly, and go on learning, too. Because it doesn't do to make quick judgements. I've had customers in who look as though they're about to select a small charm for their granddaughter's birthday, and they've gone out the proud possessors of my best brooch or necklace.'

'I'll keep an open mind,' nodded Catherine.

'Then we'll have first break for a cup of tea, then John and Elizabeth can go. We never leave the shop unattended.'

'I can understand *that*.'

Uncle James escorted her through to a neat office at the back of the shop. It was scantily but nicely furnished, and a tray had been set out with tea and biscuits by Mrs Neal. Catherine was surprised to find that she needed that cup of tea, and they wasted no time lingering over it, even though Uncle James assured her, ruefully, that the shop was never terribly busy early in the morning.

As they went back to relieve John and Elizabeth,

35

Catherine's eye was caught by a ring of emeralds and diamonds in a very unusual design, and she paused to look at it more closely, and very admiringly. It was delicate and dainty rather than ostentatious.

'Lovely, isn't it, Miss Catherine?' asked a voice behind her, and she jumped a little, while Mrs Neal apologised for startling her.

'I didn't hear you come in.'

'It's the thick carpet.'

'I was so interested in the ring.'

Mrs Neal nodded. 'It was a very special one, that,' she confided, 'and I'm glad to see it out on show again, dear. It was Mr John's engagement ring, you see, only she gave it back to him.'

'Oh!'

Catherine felt taken aback. Somehow it had never occurred to her that John, too, might have been engaged. She wanted to ask all sorts of questions, and a look at Mrs Neal told her that she would be given all the answers, too. But she felt distaste for that kind of gossip.

'It's lovely,' she said evenly, and walked on to her own side of the shop.

'He's got over it now, I'll bet,' said Mrs Neal, determined to have the last word. 'He'll be over it when he's put the ring up for sale. He designed it himself, and had it made up. But I bet she'd rather have had the pick of the diamonds, and I expect that's why he took it back. He would be just the kind to ask her to keep it otherwise.'

Who was the girl? wondered Catherine. But Uncle James was now walking towards them, and Mrs Neal had finished the last of the cleaning. Then John and Elizabeth returned, and the first customer of the day arrived, with a watch to be mended, and soon is was Catherine's turn to deal with a charming elderly woman who was buying pearl earrings for her granddaughter's twenty-first birthday.

Catherine enjoyed selling the earrings, and thought how delighted the girl was going to be. She herself had a beautiful brooch in freshwater pearls for her twenty-first birthday, the last gift from her father before he died. She treasured it above anything she possessed, and she decided to ask Elizabeth if she could wear it pinned to her plain dark blue dress.

But she forgot all about asking Elizabeth. That afternoon the shop door clanged, and a tall, very dark young man strode in purposefully. Catherine looked up and her startled eyes met his, so that for a moment it seemed as though everything stood still.

Then she heard Elizabeth's glad voice.

'Michael! So you're back earlier than you expected.'

He nodded, his eyes still on Catherine, then he turned to smile at Elizabeth.

'Got through it all quite quickly. How is everything . . . and everyone?'

He glanced again at Catherine, and Elizabeth quickly introduced them.

'You remember, Father told you about Catherine

before you left.'

'Of course. How do you do? I hope you'll be happy here.'

Catherine could only nod and smile. She thought that Elizabeth's fiancé was one of the handsomest men she had ever met, and he had that peculiar magnetic quality which both attracted and repelled her.

Then she looked at Elizabeth whose unusual features were suddenly radiant, and she changed her mind about Elizabeth's looks. Now she was beautiful.

That evening Catherine felt very tired as she crawled into bed, though for a long time sleep eluded her. It had been an exciting day. She had enjoyed working at Sheridan and Rodgers, and she could see again some of the lovely pieces of jewellery displayed for sale, pieces which she had examined quite closely as they were put in the safe for the night.

She thought again about the pretty ring which John had packed away with the others. Had his hand trembled a little when he picked it up, and had she only imagined Michael Rodgers' slightly raised eyebrows, and Elizabeth's warning frown when he caught sight of it. What had his fiancée been like, and why had she returned the ring? Questions chased themselves round in Catherine's head as she tossed and turned. John had seemed quieter and older in the atmosphere of the large shop, and she wondered how well he and Michael Rodgers got on together.

Catherine closed her eyes again, aware that almost for the first time in weeks her last thoughts weren't of her mother and Philip, and the usual familiar throb of pain whenever she thought about them was considerably dulled. Perhaps, soon, she would be able to think about them with love, in the same way as she remembered her father.

But it was Michael Rodgers' striking good looks which dominated her thoughts when she finally fell asleep. He had gazed at her searchingly, as though weighing her up, then he had almost ignored her entirely. He and Uncle James had disappeared into the office, no doubt while Michael told him all about the new designs in clocks and watches he recommended for purchase.

Or did Michael do his own purchasing? Catherine had no idea, and as her eyes grew heavy, it did not seem to be important.

CHAPTER III

Catherine began to settle down to a new routine, and very soon she could price any particular string of pearls, and only needed to examine the ticket to confirm that price.

Uncle James was a born teacher, and began to tell her about gold and platinum, then on to the precious stones such as emeralds, diamonds, rubies and sapphires, teaching her the relative hardness of each stone compared to the diamond which is the hardest of all known stones, and how to test for specific gravity and refractive index, or the angle at which a ray of light is bent when it hits the surface of a stone.

She learned how to distinguish between the various cuts of stones, the brilliant cut from the rose, the step cut from the marquise. She learned, too, that sometimes emeralds, sapphires and rubies were more beautiful in a polished form, cabochon cut, than the brilliant cut.

'Look at these stones,' Uncle James told her, spreading out one or two diamonds big enough to take Catherine's breath away. 'How much would you give me for that one?'

'Oh, Uncle James, I couldn't guess. It's fabulous!'

'Look again, my dear,' he said quietly, and

Catherine took another look. Wasn't it just a little too brilliant, too perfect? she wondered, and frowned.

'Is . . . is it *really* a diamond?'

'Why do you ask?'

'It . . . well, it seems brighter, somehow.'

He smiled broadly, well pleased.

'It's a new form of simulated diamond, the closest ever to the diamond which man has produced himself. In a smaller stone, I guess even I would have to look twice and then look again.'

'Then isn't it just as good? I mean wouldn't a ring set with that stone be just as wonderful, and a lot less costly than a diamond ring?'

'Perhaps. But then it wouldn't be a diamond, would it? It would always just have simulated diamond value. Do you prefer the cultured pearls to the ones your father found?'

She shook her head, smiling.

'Why not?'

'Oh, I don't know. They're different somehow, even though cultured pearls are still made by the oyster.'

Uncle James was smiling again.

'Yes, my dear, they're different. Now take these books home. I'll find out about classes for you, in order that you can learn how to use such things as a refractometer. John can help us there. I'd like you to stick at it, if you can, Catherine. It's what your father would have wished, I'm sure. Oh, by the way, now that your flat has been let, and all your personal items gathered together, would you like the rest of them brought here? Do you feel settled enough to stay, Catherine?'

She nodded. Her life still seemed rather strange to her, and oddly unreal, but she was more settled here, with something interesting to do, than she would have been in Perth. Uncle James had quickly arranged the storage of her best furniture, and she herself had already packed away all her own personal possessions, and had a box full of private papers and other small items belonging to her parents.

Soon, when she felt able to tackle the job, she would have to go through everything. All bills had been paid, and she had also been to see the family solicitor and bank manager, feeling grateful that there was a small amount of money, but not enough to allow her to forget about the future.

Sometimes it stretched before her like a great void, and she would feel sudden panic if her head ached again, as it often did since the accident. What would happen to her in the case of illness? Suppose she couldn't look after herself properly? Her small nest-egg would seem very small indeed, and she would feel frightened and insecure.

It was then that she often wished that her mother had been willing to discuss their true financial position with her, but ever since her father had died so suddenly, her mother had taken all responsibility on to her own shoulders, and had managed their affairs herself. Even when she was on holiday, everything had been organised for Catherine in her absence.

Catherine's heart contracted a little when she thought, too, of her father. He had been older than Alison by fifteen years, and she remembered her mother's anxiety after they had paid a visit to a heart specialist in Edinburgh just a few months before he died.

David Lyall had been poor at following his doctor's advice, and he had continued to lead a rich, full life. A few days before he died, he had hurried off to London on business, and had called in to see the Sheridans on his way back home. Catherine had taken a telephone call from Newcastle, and her father had sounded well and strong, and full of his usual enthusiasm for life. But the excitement of that trip must have cost him his life, because the following morning he had fallen as soon as he got out of bed, and Alison had shouted for Catherine to ring the doctor.

It was too late. David Lyall died suddenly, and after Alison's grief had subsided, she was glad it happened that way.

' He hated the thought of being an invalid,' she told Catherine. ' It's better this way . . . for him.'

Now there was only Catherine, and a large box full of old papers, boxes of old-fashioned trinkets which had belonged to both grandmothers, then her mother, old precious books and small pieces of silver which Catherine wanted to keep. Some furniture had stayed in the flat, and some had gone into store against the day when she might once again have her own home. Somehow that day seemed very far away. It was a day she might dream about, though the dream was too cloudy to seem anything like reality.

In the meantime, she could only be grateful for the home which had been given to her.

It was a few days before Catherine managed to exchange more than half a dozen words with Michael Rodgers. After the first warm handshake, he had treated her very formally in the shop, though she recognised that he seemed to be kept busy with his part of the business.

New ranges of watches and clocks had been ordered, and he rearranged the window display to show off the best designs to greatest advantage. He and Elizabeth seemed to work well together, though occasionally there would be a difference of opinion, when Elizabeth's eyes would flash and her chin lift a little. It seemed to be only in this particular field that she stood up to Michael. She knew her job, and although Catherine knew too little about the business to judge, she often felt that Elizabeth was in the right. It was then that Michael would often be the peacemaker.

44

'All right, all right, darling, don't get het up. We'll have it your way.'

Then Elizabeth would bite her lip.

'I know I'm right, Michael.'

'All right. I've agreed you're right.'

On Saturday Mrs Sheridan asked Elizabeth if Michael would be coming home with them that evening for dinner.

'I . . . I think so,' she said, a trifle doubtfully.

'Won't you be going out together, darling?'

'Michael didn't mention his plans. I'll see what he wants to do.'

'What about you, John, and Catherine?'

'I rather think Catherine will be too tired to do more than crawl home,' said John, with one of his teasing smiles in Catherine's direction. 'Or do you want to dance all night, Kate?'

'No, thanks,' she laughed. 'If Saturdays are as busy as you say, then I shan't want to go anywhere.'

'Then we'll come straight home, if we may, Mother. I'll take Catherine out for a drive this Sunday. She's more acclimatised now, and an outing to Housesteads would do her good. She can see something of the Roman Wall.'

'Oh, but . . .'

'All you'll have to do is sit in the car, and you must have a break of sorts. You'll soon get your sea legs.'

'Then thank you, John,' she accepted gratefully. 'It's nice of you to bother about me.'

'It's a pleasure,' said John, and she saw that this time his eyes were serious, and he said it as though he meant it. He was really a nice person, she thought, studying him. In fact, she had considered him to be very good-looking until Michael Rodgers walked into the shop. Michael's looks were much more flamboyant.

During the morning she heard Elizabeth ringing home and telling her mother to expect Michael for dinner. Catherine suddenly felt rather less tired. There would be six for dinner that evening. She didn't know why that pleased her, but she thought it might be rather interesting. She wondered what Michael Rodgers would be like as a person away from the atmosphere of Sheridan and Rodgers.

That evening Catherine changed out of her plain everyday dress into a softly feminine one in a shade of blue which made her eyes look like the brightest sapphires. She brushed up her dark hair into curls on her small head, and clipped on her lovely pearl brooch.

She was beginning to look better, she thought, studying her own reflection in the full-length mirror in her room. There was fresh colour in her cheeks, and her eyes looked brighter now that the dull lifeless feeling was beginning to lift from her heart.

Obviously Elizabeth thought so, too, because she paused for a moment at the top of the stairs as Catherine came out of her room, and looked at the other girl appraisingly.

'You must have made a special effort tonight, Catherine,' she said lightly, though there was a slightly jagged note in the words.

She herself was very smart in a turquoise trouser suit, which looked perfect on her slim boyish figure and contrasted with the red glow of her hair.

'I haven't your flair, Elizabeth,' Catherine returned honestly, and for a moment the other girl's eyes softened, and she took Catherine's arm as they walked downstairs.

'Do you still miss your fiancé?' she asked, and felt Catherine stiffen a little. Time was healing, but now and again a jarring note would bring it all back to her.

'Yes, I do,' she said briefly, and the other girl gave her arm a small squeeze.

'Don't let anyone catch you on the rebound,' she advised. 'One can do foolish things out of . . . loneliness, perhaps . . .'

'I hardly think there's any fear of that,' Catherine told her, with a rueful smile. 'Have you and Michael been engaged long, Elizabeth? Are you being married soon?'

This time Elizabeth became rather more withdrawn.

'We've been engaged for over a year,' she said flatly. 'Michael has commitments which will have to be resolved before we fix the wedding date.'

'Oh,' said Catherine. She felt as though she had

been treading on private ground, and it was obvious that Elizabeth had no wish to discuss anything further with her. She crossed to the lounge and threw open the door where James Sheridan seemed to be arguing with his son and Michael. All three men stood up briefly, and again Catherine felt uncomfortable. She could see the small, rather twisted smile on John's face, while Michael looked very cool and remote. Uncle James's colour was rather high, but he forced a smile when he saw the two girls.

'Oh, hello, you two. Is it time, then?'

'Yes, come along, all of you,' said Aunt Lucille, coming into the room behind them. 'We're all ready to begin.'

Michael had taken Elizabeth's arm, but his eyes lingered on Catherine and she was again fully aware of his attraction, as John came over and took her arm, grinning down at her.

'Someone looks lovely tonight,' he told her admiringly, and she felt her cheeks colour. As John walked beside her, she was aware of his rather quick breathing, and a glance confirmed her suspicions. In spite of his friendly greeting, and his smile, John was seething with anger, and she could sense the power in him which made even Michael seem less striking. What had been said to make him so annoyed? she wondered. She suspected more and more that all was not well in the relationship between the three men.

Could Michael be standing on his rights as a junior

48

partner against the other two? Or was it the two younger men who were all out to modernise and move with the times, against tradition?

Now and again she had heard John advocate a more modern approach for some things, and to argue amiably with his father, who maintained that customers liked to be conservative about their jewellery.

'If they pay a lot of money for something, they want to be sure it isn't a gimmicky thing which will go out of fashion in a year,' he argued. 'They want something which is going to last and last.'

'But fashions do change, Father,' John had argued. 'I mean, just look at some of this second-hand Victorian stuff we've got in to sell. It's nothing like our present-day stock, yet people are buying it all over again. Fashions do keep changing, but people aren't going to throw their jewellery away just because it goes out of fashion. They'll keep it, because it's sure to be back *in* fashion again.'

'Only good stuff that lasts. Some of that stuff is just rubbish. These Victorian pieces are of good design. Probably there was rubbish then, too, but it will have vanished long ago.'

John sighed, then shrugged with his usual grin.

'All right. You're still the boss.'

'Good job, too!'

Uncle James had grinned at Catherine. She had a feeling they enjoyed their squabbles, but it looked as though they had not enjoyed the last one.

However, the atmosphere at the dinner table

lightened a little as Mrs Bannon passed round plates and Aunt Lucille talked lightly of the happenings of the day. She had been chairman at a Spring Fête for one of her pet charities, and a local artist had opened the Fête.

'He's a wonderful artist, but an appalling speaker,' said Aunt Lucille. 'Everything he said had a double meaning, and the hall rocked with laughter. He was very surprised, and it was all rather embarrassing.'

'I should have thought it was a howling success, Mother,' John commented, his eyes dancing.

'Well, it wasn't at all as it was meant to be,' said Aunt Lucille, and Uncle James, too, began to chuckle.

'What did he say?'

'You should have been there to hear,' Aunt Lucille told him pointedly. 'I told you the children could manage on their own for one day.'

'Children!' shrieked John and Elizabeth in chorus.

This time Michael caught Catherine's glance across the table, and she saw that he, too, was beginning to laugh a little.

'*Not* on a Saturday,' said Uncle James firmly.

'Well, all right. But I refuse to satisfy your curiosity by repeating the speech.'

'I had a funny woman in today who showed me a ring she had bought from the fashion jewellery counter of a large store. A friend was sure a mistake had been made and the stones were real, and she wanted me to confirm this, and buy it back from her! I kept trying to tell her it was only paste, but her friend had known better, and I just couldn't convince her. She went off in a huff, no doubt to try someone else. Some people are odd about their jewellery. If anyone suggests their piece is valuable, then nothing will convince them that it isn't.'

'It's like that with watches sometimes,' agreed Michael. 'They won't believe that a watch can wear out after years of faithful service. The same old watch keeps coming back again and again for repair, and they can become rather offended if one suggests that it's suffering from old age. It kept perfect time for Grandfather, so why not now?'

'Must my family always talk shop?' asked Lucille. 'Let's go through to the drawing room for coffee, shall we?'

'Of course, my dear,' said James. 'Then perhaps you'll give us that speech by your artist friend!'

In the drawing room Catherine found herself sitting next to Michael on a large, rather sumptuous couch, while Elizabeth had plumped herself down on the other side, then jumped up again, excusing herself to go and find her handkerchief. James had taken John into the study for a moment, and Catherine found, to her slight discomfort, that she and Michael were alone.

'Oh. Perhaps I'd better see if I can help Aunt

Lucille with anything,' she said confusedly.

'Oh, must you? Surely everyone can't desert me, or I shall think I have B.O. or something.' His dark eyes suddenly glinted rather wickedly into hers. 'Besides, I don't think I've yet said hello properly to you, and that I'm glad to have you with us.'

'Thank you,' she said, faint colour in her cheeks. 'I was hoping you wouldn't think I was in the way. I mean, sometimes I feel that I've been rather foisted on Sheridan and Rodgers, and you, being a Rodgers, might have resented me since it was the Sheridans who brought me here.'

'The thought never occurred to me,' Michael told her. 'Besides . . .'

'What?'

'I doubt if I'd have been consulted, anyway,' he told her, with a small laugh.

'Oh, but surely, since you're a partner . . .'

He glanced at her, frowning. 'I'm the son of James Sheridan's partner,' he said flatly. 'I've no more authority than . . .'

'John?'

'Perhaps. You're David Lyall's daughter, aren't you? The pearl man.'

'Yes, but my parents are dead now, and I . . . well, I'm having to work for my living.'

'Not exactly for your living, surely. Not with your father fishing out pearls.'

She laughed. 'And you a jeweller! I would have thought you would know that it isn't all that easy to find really wonderful pearls, enough to become rich.'

'No, but . . .' He glanced at her curiously. 'Never mind. I think Elizabeth said her father had been made your guardian or something.'

'He's my godfather, though we haven't really seen much of the Sheridans over the years. My father kept in touch, and called in when he went to London on business. It's awfully good of Uncle James and Aunt Lucille to give me a home like this.'

'What were you doing otherwise?'

'I had a flat in Perth, but Uncle James has seen to it all for me. It's been let and the things I want to keep are in store.'

'In store in Perth?'

'Yes, though I've a few boxes and cases to go through here. I keep putting it off, but I'll have to start to it all one of these days. I . . . I'm only getting my sea legs back after . . . after the accident,' she said, a trifle shakily.

'Poor Catherine!' His eyes had grown rather soft as he looked down at her.

'Oh, it's all right,' she said hastily. 'I'm tons better now. Coming here has helped enormously.'

'I've no doubt,' he said, rather dryly. 'They'll make you very welcome. But don't go grovelling with gratitude. Take it from me, there's no need.'

His voice was suddenly harsh, and she felt an odd twinge of distaste when she looked up into his dark, moody face. This man was an enigma to her. He could be bright and charming, then in a moment she could feel an almost sulky moodiness in him, and a sort of smouldering anger. Against whom? At first she had wondered if it could be herself, but now she knew it wasn't. Yet it would appear that Michael Rodgers had everything which should bring happiness to a young man . . . good looks, a share in a fine, well established business, and someone as attractive and suitable as Elizabeth for his fiancée. He seemed to be welcomed into the Sheridan family, so what could be wrong?

'Do you like being a jeweller?' she asked suddenly, and he relaxed.

'Love it,' he told her briefly. 'I've always been interested in clocks and watches ever since my grandfather used to hold his big hunter watch to my ear to listen to the ticking. Then I often watched my father taking a clock to pieces for mending. . . .'

He broke off abruptly, and she saw the dark look coming back over his face. It was some years now since his father had died. Perhaps he had been at a difficult age for a boy to lose someone he loved.

Catherine felt her heart soften towards this dark man who, she felt now, was hiding some sort of unrest or unhappiness. She had fellow feeling for him, having felt the same empty loss herself. Perhaps Elizabeth could give him her love, but be unable to give him complete understanding over this. As yet she had been untouched by unhappiness of this sort, being a treasured member of a loving family.

Catherine put her fingers light on his arm.

'You must miss him,' she said softly, and was unaware of her own beauty, her face soft with compassion. Michael stared at her, and in that moment Elizabeth and John walked in, followed by Uncle James and Lucille.

The spell was broken, though for some reason Catherine felt oddly shaken and could only be aware of the magnetic quality of Michael's eyes as they held hers.

Then, as though douched with cold water, she became aware of Elizabeth and John both staring at her, and she felt chastened. Surely Elizabeth could not imagine that she had been trying to . . . to catch Michael's interest. Or John either.

She sat back, confused, and was glad when the two older people started a new conversation, and she only need sit and listen. Elizabeth needn't be jealous, she wanted to assure her. She could never attract Michael Rodgers while Elizabeth was around, and anyway, she wouldn't dream of such a thing. She wasn't the sort of girl to go round stealing other people's boy-friends. Her heart had been given to Philip Neill.

The memory of Philip was beginning to fade a little. She still loved him, but it was gradually becoming the love of memory. Though she was far from falling in love with anyone else, Catherine assured herself. And certainly not with Michael Rodgers.

CHAPTER IV

On Sunday the cold weather of early spring suddenly vanished, and Catherine woke to warm sunshine and a new surge of life in the loud chorussing of the birds, and the bleating of new lambs in distant fields.

She threw open her bedroom window feeling some of the abundant youthful energy returning to her limbs, after the many weeks of lethargy following her accident.

Today John was taking her to Housesteads, which had been a Roman fort, now being excavated. Catherine had a passion for old ruins of this kind, and liked to allow her imagination to run riot as she looked at ancient buildings, and thought about the sort of people who had built them, and lived in them so long ago.

John had warned her to go warmly clad, in spite of the sunshine, against the winds which blew across the great open spaces. She chose a russet-coloured trouser suit and stout brogues, so that she could cope with any climbing which might have to be done. Then she combed up her long soft dark hair into a topknot, and pinned it securely.

Excitement had brought colour to her cheeks, so that Mrs Bannon smiled on her approvingly when she ran down into the large kitchen where a breakfast table was set in the window.

'You're beginning to look a lot better, Miss Catherine. I hope you've brought down a decent appetite. If so, it's more than can be said for Miss Elizabeth, who only wants a cup of coffee, and her thin enough already, goodness knows.'

Elizabeth looked up rather tiredly.

'Hello, Kate. Full of the joys of the morning, I see.'

Catherine coloured at the edge in the other girl's voice.

'John . . . John said he'd take me to Housesteads,' she said, stammering a little.

'Oh, I see.' Elizabeth pursed her lips, then she smiled a little. 'Enjoy yourselves,' she said, quite kindly.

'It should be nice, though . . .' Catherine looked round. 'I hope John hasn't forgotten. Maybe he doesn't really want to go today.'

'Who could forget an important date like that?' asked John, appearing at the kitchen door.

He, too, was clad in corduroy jeans and a warm pullover, and he carried a brown anorak over his arm, draping it carelessly over a chair.

'Hello, Kate. You look well. I hope you've stoked up with breakfast. It's a lovely day, but just wait till the chilly winds off the hills and moors get hold of you. You'll be glad you ate your porridge then.'

'Well, you eat yours, Mr John,' said Mrs Bannon, behind him, as she set down a large bowl of steaming

57

porridge.

'Ugh!' said Elizabeth.

'Stop wrinkling your nose,' John advised. 'You'll get crows' feet.'

'That's on eyes, silly!'

Catherine sat smiling, amused. She often enjoyed the exchange between brother and sister. It was rare for them to have a serious argument, and she often thought how lucky Elizabeth was to have a brother. What a difference it might have made in her own life if only she'd had someone like John. She smiled at him, her eyes soft, and he turned away from her rather abruptly. Then he settled down to eat his breakfast, insisting that Catherine should drink one more cup of coffee. Elizabeth refused anything more, saying she hadn't time.

'Where are you off to?' asked John.

'Michael and I have a date,' she said flatly.

'And we must keep our noses out of it.'

'Yes.' For a moment Elizabeth hesitated. 'Oh, all right. We're just going to look at some new houses being put up in rather a nice district. I was just thinking it was time we fixed a date for the wedding.'

She looked almost defiantly at Catherine, who again felt slightly chilled as she sensed hostility.

'I hope you find something suitable,' she said in a low voice.

'I've no doubt we shall.'

'Find what?' asked her mother, padding into

the kitchen in pretty bedroom slippers while Uncle James brought up the rear.

' A house, darling,' said Elizabeth. ' Somewhere to live. For Michael and me.'

' Michael and I,' said John.

' Michael and *me*,' corrected Elizabeth. ' Your grammar's worse than mine.'

' Are we arranging the wedding soon, then, dear?' asked Lucille. ' It's about time. You're beginning to look like an old married couple already.'

The words had been teasingly spoken and not intended to hurt, but Catherine caught sight of a flash of pain on Elizabeth's face. Maybe Aunt Lucille had touched a tender spot. She felt a sudden rush of feeling for the other girl, and touched her arm as they made for the door.

' Have a lovely day,' she said, and was surprised by the sudden glint of tears in Elizabeth's eyes, though she did not reply.

Catherine watched her running upstairs, then John's hand was on her elbow, a picnic hamper in his other hand.

' Come on, Kate hinny,' he said. ' Time we were off.'

' Kate what?'

He grinned.

'Kate, my love,' he said, his eyes dancing, and she couldn't stop the colour from again flooding her cheeks.

' Stop leg-pulling,' she said, a trifle crossly.

'Will I need anything else?'

'You're perfect as you are. And who said I was leg-pulling?'

Catherine began to feel full of well-being as they took the Hexham road out of Newcastle. John had decided that they must have a look at the lovely old town on the way to Housesteads.

'We'll come back along the Military Road,' he told her. 'Absolutely straight. If the Romans wanted to go from A to B, they went from A to B, and not via C.'

'Perhaps they had all the lie of the land to choose from,' suggested Catherine. 'Later people found they had to skirt fields when making roads, or the owner wouldn't like it.'

'And now we're back to Roman days when the owners aren't asked. Or at least, aren't considered to such an extent.'

'I hope you haven't brought your soapbox,' said Catherine. 'I used to get enough of that from Daddy. He had all his own ideas about everything.'

They were silent for a while, as John drove through the sunlit countryside where the faint green of spring was beginning to appear on the trees. It was like the surge of rebirth, and in a small way Catherine could feel it all being reflected in her own heart. She was really feeling alive again, even if it meant flashes of pain as well as happiness.

'You miss him a lot,' said John.

'Yes.'

'Did he confide in you as well as your mother?'

She felt faintly surprised by the question.

'Only about general things. If you mean business, then he kept that part of his life separate. I . . . I suppose that's why we felt so lost when he died, though it was Mother who took over. She was splendid, though it almost went for her nerves. She had to go away on holiday after I got engaged to Philip. She saw that I was settled and happy first of all. I . . . I can hardly believe it's all gone now.'

She felt John's firm fingers reaching for her own slender hand, and was comforted. Then he was again concentrating on his driving.

'Here's Hexham coming up,' he said, after a while. 'We'll park the car, then wander about. We can have a look at the ancient Abbey, if you like, one of the oldest in the country.'

It was relaxing to wander round the lovely old town, John's fingers still linking hers. Then they went into the Abbey where Catherine felt strangely awed, and very conscious of the great age of the place.

'It's awfully impressive,' she said to John, then shivered a little, 'but rather cold.'

'We'll go back to the car and have a cup of Banny's coffee and a sandwich before going on to Housesteads. Will that do?'

'Fine,' she laughed. She felt suddenly warmly protected as they hurried back to the car and shared

61

out the coffee.

'I'd like to come again another day,' she said, looking out at Hexham as they left the old town.

'I thought you would,' he grinned. 'It's the sort of place to which people do come back. Mother was born here, of course, and christened in the Abbey.'

'Oh. I didn't know.'

'We used to visit our grandparents quite often, but they're dead now. No one left in Hexham.'

Catherine was quiet on the way to Housesteads, and against her will her thoughts were turning to Elizabeth and Michael. Were they, even now, deciding on their future home, and would the strange dark moods which seemed to smoulder in Michael be dispelled? Perhaps the happiness of marriage with Elizabeth would chase them away. She could almost feel his magnetic presence, making John a more shadowy figure even though he sat beside her.

Then she gave herself a vigorous mental shake-up. Michael was beginning to disturb her far too much. She must stop thinking about him, even if the thoughts were only curiosity, and a sort of deep interest. It was up to Elizabeth to worry about him, and to ensure that he was happy. It might be dangerous if she started worrying about him.

Dangerous! The word had leapt to her mind, and she drew back, shivering again.

'I told you you'd feel chilled,' said John at her side. 'We'll soon be at Housesteads. Wrap that blanket round your knees in the meantime.'

'Thank you, John,' she said meekly.

It was exhilarating to walk up the hill to the excavated site of a Roman fort.

John took Catherine into the Museum first of all, and they examined with deep interest all the fragments of Roman pottery and utensils which had been found, then they wandered over the site, trying to imagine what it had been like in Roman times.

'Just think they had baths here, and were probably far more advanced in hygiene than some of our more recent ancestors,' said Catherine.

'Careful!' said John, grabbing her arm as she stumbled a little, then hanging on to it as he escorted her up to the Roman Wall. 'Want to walk along it for a short distance?' he asked, and she nodded.

The wind had whipped high colour into her cheeks and her eyes sparkled. John put his arm round her shoulders, then they walked in single file along the wall, until Catherine began to feel slightly giddy.

'But you can't fall off!' cried John.

'I know, but I get vertigo so easily,' she apologized. 'Can we go back now, John?'

'Of course, dear. I'm glad we saved that last cup of coffee each. I'll buy some chocolate when we get back down to the road.'

They took their time as they went back through the ancient fort, then began to descend the gentle slope.

'It's been fun,' Catherine told him. 'Thank you for bringing me.'

'We'll do it again soon,' John promised. 'Not to come here, I mean, but to go somewhere else. You must get to know Northumberland, Kate, if you're going to stay here.'

'I can't stay for ever,' she told him.

'Why not? Are you only marking time till you go back to Scotland?'

'I've no plans, and I certainly can't go back to Scotland. But I can't stay with your family for ever either, John.'

He said nothing for a while.

'Are you happy enough with us, Kate? Don't mind Elizabeth if she's a bit sharp at times. She's in love with Mike Rodgers, and can get a bit jealous, especially about a girl as lovely as you.'

Catherine blushed. 'I'm sure there's no need,' she said stiffly.

'It might be none of your doing,' John told her, 'but Mike might find it hard not to admire you at times. It . . . you would find it easy to encourage him.'

Catherine's eyes began to sparkle with annoyance.

'You're wrong, John. I'm sure you're wrong. I have no intention of encouraging Michael, and . . . and Elizabeth, and I'm quite sure he . . . he isn't the sort of man to forget that he's engaged, and to start showing interest in other girls.'

'Don't fly off the handle coming to his defence,' said John mildly. 'Only go easy with Michael. You don't know what he is . . . yet.'

'He can't be without integrity or you wouldn't want Elizabeth to marry him.'

John's face became expressionless.

'Perhaps I don't want Elizabeth to marry him,' he said, very quietly. 'Not now that . . .'

'What?'

'Nothing.'

'You can't keep your sister in a glass case.'

'Why should I want to? Of course I'd like to see her happily married, but I just don't know that it's Michael Rodgers, that's all. Only I'm in the minority, and she's over age, so I can only stand by and hope she knows what she's doing.'

They got into the car, and John busied himself by reaching for the hamper, and pouring out more coffee. It warmed Catherine again, and she began to feel the inner shakiness recede, so that she faced John more calmly. He was very fond of Elizabeth, and no doubt they'd been playmates as children. Perhaps all brothers who really cared about their sisters were inclined to want a very high standard from the men with whom they fell in love. She didn't really know.

Yet John had also fallen in love, judging by the pretty ring which was now back in stock. Had Elizabeth been similarly critical of his fiancée?

Catherine shook her head. They were a very ordinary brother and sister, and probably only concerned for each other's happiness.

'Why don't you feel that Michael is right for

Elizabeth?' she asked bluntly. 'Is it because you feel he doesn't care for her enough?'

'I don't know,' said John, more slowly. 'We've known him since he was a boy. He and I never got on, so perhaps I'm prejudiced. He took his time before making up his mind to marry Elizabeth and I can never fathom out just how much he cares for her.'

'Perhaps he wanted to be sure of offering her a nice home,' suggested Catherine, then remembered that Michael was a partner, and would be just as well placed as John in the firm, with an equally big income.

'Perhaps,' John was agreeing. 'Kate! This is in confidence. I don't want the family to know I feel this way . . . yet!'

'Of course,' she said stiffly. Did he think her some sort of telltale?

He was laughing gently as he took her coffee cup and put it away in the hamper, then suddenly he pulled her into his arms and hugged her against the soft wool of his pullover, which smelled of peat.

'Don't be such a pincushion, love. Every word I say seems to offend you. We'll kiss and be friends.'

He kissed her thoroughly, and she broke away, her eyes even more bright.

'Don't do that, John! I hate being kissed casually.'

'Do you call that casually?' he asked, eyebrows
66

shooting up.

'Well, it wasn't because you care about me. I know about . . .'

'About what?' he asked, very softly.

'Nothing.'

'I don't believe you. Only don't go listening to gossip, love. You'll only get hold of the wrong end of the stick. I can tell you all you want to know.'

'I don't! I don't want to hear about your private affairs.'

John withdrew his arm.

'Very well,' he said becoming matter-of-fact. 'Let's go home.'

They drove most of the way in silence, and Catherine felt rather lost, as though she no longer had her sense of well-being. But whether it was because she no longer felt at ease with John, or because he had forced her to be wary of Michael, she didn't quite know.

On Monday Miss Pryce returned to work, and smiled rather frostily when Catherine and she were introduced.

'How do you do, Miss Lyall. I hope you haven't been finding things difficult taking over at short notice. Especially when your experience is rather . . . limited.'

'I've enjoyed it,' Catherine told her, 'and no doubt my experience will improve with time.'

'One is learning all the time. Even I, after so

67

many years, have to be careful what I'm about. I've seen lots of changes in the firm over the years. People come and go.'

Catherine felt very transient, but she only smiled and nodded.

'Mr Sheridan must be pleased to have your services,' she said politely, and Miss Pryce unbent a little, and smiled on her kindly.

'I think he is,' she agreed, 'though he's lucky to have young Michael. John, too, of course.'

Catherine noticed that she had put Michael first, and she could see by the way the older woman glanced over at the dark-haired man that she was fond of Michael Rodgers.

'You would know his father, of course,' she put in.

'Yes,' said Miss Lyall, with a small sigh. 'I knew his father very well.'

'Hello, Prycey,' said Elizabeth, arriving a few minutes late. 'How do you feel? Able to cope?'

'As always, Elizabeth,' said Miss Pryce.

The day did not go very well. Catherine had taken a string of cultured pearls in for re-threading, and when the customer came in to collect them it was Miss Lyall who looked through the repair envelopes and picked it out.

Opening the envelope, she lifted out the pearls, and spread them on a black velvet pad.

'Those aren't mine,' the woman said. 'Mine was a longer string of pearls than that.'

68

Miss Pryce paused and compared the repair ticket numbers. On check-up, there was only one other lot of pearls in for repair and it was a double rope.

'I'm afraid these must be yours,' she insisted gently. 'Sometimes they do look different when they are re-threaded, and these ones have been done very carefully, as you can see.'

'With some of the pearls missing,' the woman insisted. 'I tell you, mine was much longer than that.'

Miss Pryce's lips compressed a little, then she asked the woman to wait while Catherine served a customer with small pearl stud earrings, then she asked her to come over, after her customer had gone.

'Did you take this necklace for repair, Miss Lyall?'

'Yes, I did,' said Catherine readily. 'You had broken it, hadn't you, madam? Doesn't it look nice now?'

'Now it's practically a choker,' the woman said coldly. 'I brought in a decent necklace of graduated pearls. A great many of them seem to be missing.'

Catherine's mouth opened, then she bit her lip. The necklace had only been half threaded, the remaining pearls loose in an envelope. It was difficult to tell how big the necklace was likely to have been.

'We have sent out our pearls to the same firm

for years,' Miss Pryce was saying, ' and they have never let us down, nor are they likely to make a mistake with the system we use for sending out repairs.'

' I should like to see someone in authority,' the customer told them firmly.

Only Michael was available, as John was busy with a couple buying an engagement ring, and Uncle James was having a late lunch. Miss Pryce explained the position to Michael, who asked the woman to come through to the office after he had questioned Catherine.

' Did you count those pearls?' he asked her, and her heart sank as she slowly shook her head.

' Did no one tell you to count the pearls carefully before the customer, and ask her to agree that you have the correct number?'

Again Catherine shook her head, her cheeks crimson. Her own common sense should have told her, but she had not thought of it.

' I suppose I can't blame you entirely, being new,' he told her, rather bitingly, ' but I shall have a word with Elizabeth later.'

He walked away towards the office and Catherine turned to Miss Lyall, appalled. For a brief moment she thought she saw a gleam of satisfaction in the older woman's eyes.

' What's Elizabeth got to do with it? It was my mistake.'

' Elizabeth should have warned you,' Miss Lyall

said. ' I should have done . . . if I'd been here.'

' Surely she can't be expected to remember to tell me everything. Some things one must pick up for oneself.'

' But not something where the customer is likely to try it on.'

' Is she trying it on?'

' I'm quite sure she is. I doubt if Michael will shake her either. We'll be out of pocket, I'm afraid, Miss Lyall. She'll want compensation for the missing pearls, and . . . of course . . . no charge for the re-threading.'

' Oh!'

Catherine's heart grew heavier. She could, perhaps, offer to pay for her mistake, but could she afford it? Not only that, but wouldn't Uncle James be very angry with her? And if it made trouble between Michael and Elizabeth, wouldn't the other girl be more than angry?

Elizabeth had been rather quiet during the week-end, after her house-hunting trip with Michael, and when Catherine had asked, with friendly interest, if she'd had a successful day, she had answered rather shortly, and Catherine had felt snubbed.

Later Elizabeth had relented, and came to smile with apology at the other girl.

' We didn't find what we wanted,' she said. ' Better luck next time, I suppose.'

' Oh, what a pity,' said Catherine. She felt very real sympathy for the other girl, whose happiness seemed to have dimmed a little. She hoped Elizabeth and Michael hadn't had a difference of opinion.

The customer left, looking annoyed and far from satisfied, and Michael beckoned for Catherine to come into the office.

'I think I convinced the lady that she was mistaken,' he told her, his eyes gleaming. 'Her pearls were graduated. It would have been difficult to restore the balance when re-threading, if some of them had been missing.

'And anyway, I recognised her as someone who makes a habit of trying it on.'

'You mean she's tried to diddle one of you before?'

'Not one of us. It was . . . in another shop,' said Michael, then he frowned sternly again. 'I hope you'll learn from this, Catherine. As I've said before, people are odd about their jewellery. They sometimes swear that the stones have been changed in a ring. Why *should* we change stones in a ring, for goodness' sake? They think jewels have been removed from their watches, which is also ridiculous. You must be on your guard, and check that you and the customer both know the exact description of the jewellery you accept for repair.'

'Yes, Michael,' said Catherine in a small voice, and suddenly he laughed.

'Cheer up! You're doing fine.'

She looked up and smiled shakily as he grinned down at her, then Elizabeth's voice broke in on them.

'Prycey says you want me, Michael.'

'Yes, I do,' he told her crisply, and Catherine's heart sank again.

'It was my fault,' she insisted uncertainly. 'I should have used my common sense.'

'What was your fault?' asked Elizabeth.

'I didn't count some pearls that came in for repair.'

'That was stupid.'

'So was not telling her,' said Michael.

'Oh, but I must have done. Didn't I tell you?'

This time it was Elizabeth who looked discomfited, and Catherine hesitated unhappily, feeling sorry that it had all happened.

'You'd better go back, Catherine,' said Michael. 'Miss Pryce may need you.'

'Of course,' she said, and closed the office door.

She felt unhappy and dissatisfied, and she was aware that Michael Rodgers had rather a hard streak in him, and wondered what he would say to Elizabeth.

At the weekend Uncle James asked her if she felt able to go through all her personal papers, and if she needed advice over anything, he would be happy to help her.

'It may take some time, my dear, but it's got to be done.'

'I know, Uncle James,' said Catherine, 'but I

think I can tackle the job now. I think the drawers were all emptied before the furniture went into store.'

' Yes, there was nothing left. I checked everything thoroughly.'

Catherine sighed as she opened up the boxes and saw the great heaps of papers and personal objects. Her mother had just kept her father's desk as it was, even to his old pipe and tobacco jar. For a moment Catherine wondered whether she ought just to keep it all as it was, too, then she sighed again. Uncle James was quite right. She ought to know just exactly what was there. It was unlikely to yield any stocks and bonds, as all financial matters had been more carefully looked after, but neither David nor Alison Lyall had been particularly neat about personal papers, and now old letters were mixed up with receipted bills.

Catherine picked up a receipted telephone account from three years ago, and reached for a waste paper basket. There was only one way to deal with some of the papers, and that was to throw them out!

She was still busy when John looked in an hour later.

' Come and have coffee,' he advised. ' My lord, that's a pile you've got in there!'

' Old letters and things,' she said, looking up with a faint smile. ' Daddy just used to shove everything into a deep drawer in his desk, then have a gigantic tidy-up once in a blue moon.'

' Is it making you feel a bit down doing it all?'

asked John.

'Not now. I'm pretty well over it.'

'I'm glad,' said John, taking her hand and pulling her to her feet. 'Come on, my lass. You'll feel better for the break.'

There was only Aunt Lucille in the drawing room where a tray with a steaming jug of coffee, and some cups were set out on a small table. She was reading a letter from one of her friends.

'Are you still off sugar, darling?' John asked her, as he went to pour.

'Just a teeny spoonful,' she said absently. 'Come over to the fire, Kate dear. Joan Spellman is a grandmother. You remember Joan, dear?'

Catherine shook her head, smiling.

'Oh no, it's your mother who knew her well. Alison didn't keep up with many of the girls we knew. She used to leave that to me. And now Joan is a grandmother. She's beaten me to it, anyway.'

'Now you know you're in no hurry to be a grandmother,' said John teasingly, as he handed her a cup of coffee.

'I haven't much choice, have I?' asked Lucille. 'There's Elizabeth shying off from fixing a wedding date, even though she and Michael have been engaged long enough now, and you calling it off with Rosalie Craven. I saw Mrs Craven only the other day and she says Rosalie will be back from America in another week or so.'

Catherine saw John's fingers tighten, and his face

75

went hard.

'I don't know why that should interest me,' he said quietly.

'If you aren't interested, you should be. Even if you're no longer engaged, it's natural to be interested in an ex-fiancée. Isn't it, Catherine?'

Catherine did not know what to say. She could see that John had no wish to discuss his ex-fiancée, and wondered if that was because he was still in love with her.

Had she thrown him over for someone else? Yet if she had, wouldn't Aunt Lucille also have had news and gossip about her engagement or marriage to that other person?

She looked again at John, but he had turned away, and was urging her to eat another biscuit. His eyes were dark as they looked at her, then he smiled.

'Keep up your strength for sorting out all those papers.'

'Oh, are you sorting out your things, Catherine?' Lucille asked, diverted. 'Have you found it yet?'

'Found what?' asked Catherine, and surprised a look of annoyance which John directed towards his mother.

'Anything, dear,' the older woman amended hastily. 'Anything of interest, I mean.'

'Only old bills. Paid, thank goodness,' she replied, and there was a long awkward silence. She could see a muscle twitching on John's face, and knew that he was upset. Maybe he had been badly hurt by Rosalie Craven.

' I'd better get back to work,' she said lightly, putting down her coffee cup.

' Finish early and we can go and see a film. Your choice,' John offered.

' Thank you, John.'

It was a nice offer, and she was happy to take him up on it. As she closed the door she could hear John's voice, suddenly full of annoyance.

' Honestly, Mum, your tongue runs away with you at times!'

She could not hear Aunt Lucille's reply, and she walked on thoughtfully. Was that because of Rosalie, or because she had asked if Catherine had found ' it '? Found what? she wondered, then shrugged. Lucille was a very curious person. Going through a lot of personal things would no doubt give her a lot of pleasure, except, of course, if the circumstances were the same as Catherine's. No doubt that was what she had meant.

Catherine got few letters, except from Mrs Neill and a few friends she had known in Perth, but she exclaimed with pleasure when Elizabeth handed her a blue envelope with large rather scrawling writing.

' Oh, lovely! One from Janie. She never writes, either, unless she really has to.'

' Janie?' asked Aunt Lucille.

Catherine's smile wavered for a moment.

' Yes—Janie Howat. She was going to have been

my bridesmaid.'

Her voice trailed off as she read the letter, then the joy and laughter was back on her face.

'Janie's getting married. On Saturday, no less. She's dithered about writing to tell me, because . . . well, she felt I would be upset since she never was my bridesmaid. But of course I'm not. Not at all,' she added firmly.

'Of course not, dear. You'll have to choose something nice for a wedding gift. No doubt James could help you with that. . . .'

'She's wondering if I can go to the wedding.' Catherine bit her lip. 'But it's a Saturday.'

'We'd manage without you for one day now that Prycey is back,' Elizabeth told her, and Catherine restrained the impulse to hug her. Somehow Elizabeth wasn't the sort of girl one hugged. All she ever managed for her mother was a cool kiss on the cheek, and Catherine often wondered if she had saved all her love for Michael.

'It would be wonderful if I could go,' she said eagerly, and when James Sheridan came in, and gave her permission, she was delighted.

Catherine bought a new suit and hat for the wedding. She had already telephoned Mrs Neill who invited her to stay overnight until Sunday, and as Catherine travelled north on the train, she laid aside the magazines John had bought for her, and gazed out at the passing fields, and small lonely houses perched high on hillsides between each town. She had much to think about.

Recently she had been avoiding Michael Rodgers, taking care never to be alone with him. Often she would look up to find his dark eyes fixed on her, and she was becoming more and more shy of him. That he and Elizabeth were often at odds was also becoming apparent, and Catherine was conscious of tension growing in the shop which offered every sign of peace and tranquillity to its customers.

Often, too, Michael was out of the shop for fairly long periods, which caused Uncle James to frown a little. He liked to deliver the larger clocks himself, and to see them properly installed, and keeping perfect time.

' It's essential to give this service,' Michael said, ' because people trust you to do the best for them.'

' Even to sending them somewhere else when they come in to look at our range?' asked Uncle James, rather dryly, and Michael flushed a dull red.

' Yes,' he said defiantly.

' Sometimes people like to see a good variety of clocks, even if they have something special in mind,' Uncle James argued. ' It could be that something we have would have suited them much better. Only you don't always give them the opportunity, Michael. They get sent along to Newclox before you've talked to them for five minutes.'

' Maybe they send people to us, if they haven't got what a customer wants either,' argued Michael.

' Maybe.' Uncle James's tone was dry and he

stroked his upper lip thoughtfully.

'Anyway, if sales are bad, why don't you have a word with John?' asked Michael, his cheeks still flushed and his eyes sparkling.

'John?'

'Yes. He's fond of paying too high a price for secondhand pieces which people bring in. He'd get them very much cheaper if he tried.'

It was John's turn to colour.

'I give people a fair price if they want to sell any-thing,' he said, very quietly. 'We do a good trade in secondhand goods. Lots of people prefer to buy them, because there's no tax.'

'Even if new is often better cut and better set.'

'That's true, but it's people we're dealing with, and if they think they're going to be happy with an older secondhand piece, then why shouldn't they have it? Some of the pieces are lovely after I've cleaned them up. People allow their jewellery to get dirty, when they wouldn't dream of using a soiled handkerchief.'

'Even so, you won't make much profit at the prices you offer.'

'Oh, for goodness' sake!' said John crossly. 'We'll get nowhere if we keep watching one another all the time.'

'I agree,' said Michael, and James stood looking from one to the other.

'Nevertheless, things aren't going as well as they might for the firm at the moment,' he said quietly.

'I hope you'll both bear it in mind. The cost of modernising the shop, both inside and out, was considerable, and although we took a chance on modern-styled jewellery, which I have never liked myself, the public don't seem to appreciate it either.'

'Give it time,' said John. 'Those new gem stones in dialite and yttrium aluminate are doing well.'

He had been mainly responsible for trying out new ideas. He knew, though, that it was also important to stick to traditional styles, though he argued that if new designs weren't available, how would people know whether they liked them or not?

'They are selling, if slowly,' he pointed out. 'My mistake was to buy too many at the start.'

'We all make mistakes,' said James, sighing, then suddenly he smiled. 'It's good to blow off steam occasionally, though, and we certainly want new ideas. We could do with something that was completely our own. Put your minds to it, and if you come up with something worthwhile, then I'll be happy to try it. Perhaps the new gem stones might be the very thing. After all, it's in your interests, too, Michael. You'll be sharing equally in the firm when you're married to Elizabeth.'

Catherine had been unable to help overhearing the conversation. She was in the shop on her own, Elizabeth having gone for lunch, and Miss Pryce being at the bank for Uncle James. The men had been at the other side of the shop, but their voices had carried quite clearly, and although she had cleared her throat, and John had glanced in her direction, they made no attempt to walk away, or to lower their voices.

Now, sitting in the train, Catherine pondered a little. Was business so very worrying for Uncle James and John? And surely Michael had been staying out for longer than he need. Quite often both she and Elizabeth had had to help out with the watches and clocks.

She was well used to taking watches for repairs now, and showing new ones to prospective buyers. But she could not explain their relative merits to enquiring people, and unhappily, she had sometimes watched people leave without making up their minds, probably because she wasn't competent enough to make the sale. She had, rather uneasily, explained this to Michael, but he told her to think nothing of it.

' If they really want it, Catherine,' he told her, ' they'll have it, no matter what you say.'

' Oh, I hope you're right, Michael.'

She had felt the pressure of his fingers on her hand, and had quickly pulled away, and gone back to her own counter. She glanced at Elizabeth who didn't appear to notice anything, but her face looked pale and white under the bright lights of the shop, which did so much to turn the sparkling diamonds and other precious stones into some sort of fairyland.

Catherine pondered on the words she had heard. Uncle James had said Michael would be part of the firm ' when he married Elizabeth '. But surely he was part of the firm now. He was the only son of Uncle James's partner, who was now dead. Surely the partnership would then go to his only son.

Unless he had to earn his spurs. Perhaps he and John were both serving some sort of apprenticeship before they had any real responsibility in the firm . . . before they became junior partners.

Catherine gave herself a mental shake. It was none of her business what their position was with the firm. It wasn't good that her mind should keep running on Mike Rodgers, and everything which touched him.

She was glad to be going back to Perth again. There she might see things in proper perspective.

CHAPTER V

Mr and Mrs Neill were delighted to see Catherine again, and the older woman hugged her warmly. Remembering her thoughts that she might only be loved because of Philip, Catherine felt ashamed. The Neills cared about her for her own sake, and a wave of nostalgia swept over her for what she had lost.

'You're looking better, dear, isn't she?' she appealed to Mr Neill.

'You look very well, Catherine,' he told her gently, then picked up her case. 'I'll take this up to your old room for you.'

It was a weekend which Catherine was to remember because it put an end to the rather numbed feelings she had had following the loss of Philip and her mother. Now she really felt that it was all behind her.

Janie's wedding brought genuine happiness to Catherine on behalf of her friend, and the final pang for what she had lost. Though her body felt vividly alive again, and that night she wept hot, silent tears into her pillow, then fell asleep exhausted.

John was meeting her off the train when she returned, and although she had come down to breakfast with shadowed eyes and slightly swollen lids, she felt composed and at peace with herself.

'Are you happy with the Sheridans, Catherine?' asked Mrs Neill, obviously bringing herself to ask the question. Catherine was now better able to understand her rather retiring nature, and to meet it half way.

'Yes, I'm happy,' she said, after a while. 'Not completely happy, perhaps, but then there's always something, isn't there?'

'And what is there in Newcastle that worries you?'

'I don't know . . . quite,' said Catherine, slowly stirring her tea. 'I thought it would be good to come here and look at it all from a distance, but I still don't know that there's anything wrong. Yet sometimes it feels as though something is brewing up, if you know what I mean.'

Mrs Neill said nothing, but sat down at the table beside Catherine and reached for the coffee pot.

'Mr Sheridan seemed very keen to have you,' she said slowly. 'He arranged all your affairs here very well. We hardly had to do a thing. Are you being given . . . well, a lot of responsibility in his business? Too much, perhaps, for a girl like you?'

'No, nothing like that,' laughed Catherine. 'They didn't have to make a job for me, because there's plenty for us all to do. But I don't exactly run the show!'

She thought of Uncle James looking worried now and again, and knew she couldn't discuss his business with Mrs Neill.

'What are his son and daughter like?' Mrs Neill was asking. 'Are they happy to have you with them? And do you like them?'

'I think so,' said Catherine rather slowly again. 'John is always charming and thoughtful, and Elizabeth sometimes . . . sometimes I wonder if she's completely happy. It's hard to understand Elizabeth.'

And Michael Rodgers? Catherine found she could not discuss Michael with the Neills. Instead she smiled brightly.

'Everything is fine, really. I like handling pearls.'

'Even if " Pearls mean tears "?'

'That's rubbish, I'm sure. The only tears would be if one lost them!'

She began to tell the older woman some of her experiences at the shop, and soon they were both laughing, while Catherine helped to prepare Sunday lunch, then all three went walking round old haunts, and greeting old neighbours, before she caught her train back to Newcastle.

It would be nice to see John again, she thought idly, remembering his tall, rather gangling figure and his friendly teasing grin. John had been a good friend and his ex-fiancée, Rosalie Craven, must need her head examined for throwing him over like that.

And wouldn't it be nice if Elizabeth would fix a wedding date? Perhaps she might ask her to be bridesmaid. But even as the thought entered her head, more treacherous ones pushed it out. Catherine found she didn't want to be Elizabeth's bridesmaid. In fact, she was beginning to feel torn in two. She wanted the other girl to be happy, but against her will, Michael Rodgers was getting in her way. That was the cloud which was now hanging over her in Newcastle, she acknowledged honestly.

If she had any sense, she would leave the Sheridans now, before the cloud darkened and then drenched all of them.

But where would she go? A great deal of the nameless fears and insecurity she had felt after the accident, still remained with her, and Catherine didn't feel brave enough to step out, yet again, into the unknown.

Nor could she go back to Perth. Mrs Neill had confided that they were thinking of selling up their comfortable house, and moving to a small bungalow in preparation for retirement days. There would be no room in the bungalow for her, and she could little afford to be independent.

The future looked as darkened and cloudy as the sky, at the moment, she thought, as she watched the rather pale sun droop behind the skyline of jagged faraway hills.

At Newcastle she picked up her small case and smoothed down her pretty heather-coloured suit, bought specially for the wedding. She would look for John at the barrier.

But there was no sign of him as she stared round,

87

then she started as a firm hand clasped her arm.

'Here you are at last! That train was damn late. . . .'

She whirled round. 'Michael!'

He nodded, then reached for her case.

'John couldn't come. I offered to pick you up instead. Are you . . . glad to be back, Catherine?'

'Yes. Yes,' she repeated, still bewildered. 'Did Elizabeth come with you?'

'No,' he answered shortly. 'Nor did she mind my coming, if that's your next question. Elizabeth, in fact . . .'

'What?'

'Oh, nothing. Shall we go?'

Michael propelled her towards his car, and a moment later they were driving through the city, along broad well-lit streets, then suddenly turning off into a quiet cul-de-sac.

'Why are we stopping here?' she asked, in alarm.

'Why are you always so scared of me?' he countered. 'Every time I even look at you, or smile, you shy away like a startled pony. I'm not such an ogre, surely?'

She said nothing for a moment. She could hardly explain to Michael that he had a strangely deep attraction for her, and she wasn't at all sure how she felt about him.

'I . . . I'm sorry,' she managed. 'I didn't know that I seemed so unfriendly.'

'Well, I shan't labour the point, my dear,' he

said softly. ' I just thought you'd welcome a meal before going home, after your train journey. One of the hotels near here serves up a very fine steak.'

' Oh, I couldn't eat all that much!'

' An omelette then, for goodness' sake. What a difficult girl you can be!'

She relaxed and laughed a little. ' Perhaps something in between,' and he helped her out of the car and locked up, then took her arm again, and she could feel the strength of his fingers gripping her.

The hotel dining room was warm and relaxing, with old oak beams, willow-patterned plates hung on white walls, and a rich red carpet on the floor.

' There now, don't you feel hungry?' asked Michael, showing Catherine the menu.

She threw off her inhibitions and smiled at him. It was rather exciting to be having this unexpected outing, and she gave herself up to the enjoyment of it.

' It is tempting,' she agreed, as she chose fruit juice, followed by turbot, then decided that she would tackle the steak after all.

' Have you laid all your ghosts in Perth?' Michael asked suddenly, and she flushed, rather caught out by the question.

' Yes.'

' You might have been happy in the life you planned for yourself, but if fate steps in and you can't have it, there's often something just as good along a different road.'

'Perhaps that is so.'

His face darkened, and he leaned towards her.

'Sometimes one is going down the wrong road before one realises it,' he said to her. 'Often it's difficult to turn back, unless there's a hand waiting to help.'

She frowned. Was he talking about himself now?

The waitress came with their order and Michael sat back, glowering a little, and there was an awkward silence between them.

'Were you busy? Yesterday, I mean?' Catherine asked nervously.

'What? Yesterday? Oh yes. Yes, quite busy. For the moment I'd forgotten you were away.' He was silent for a while. 'It can't last for ever, though.'

'What?'

'Losing business.'

'Are we losing business?'

Michael nodded.

'James Sheridan doesn't see where the main weakness lies, because often I can cover up, but I don't think John is ever going to learn. He makes mistakes over valuations, then the firm stands the cost of his mistakes. I know one learns by experience, but in this day and age, experience can be too dearly bought.'

'I find it hard to believe . . . that John makes such serious mistakes, I mean.'

He eyed her levelly, then in a moment he was

smiling again.

' Maybe there's no point in telling you this. Maybe I'm just being pessimistic. He's a straight chap, doing his best. It's wrong of me to criticise him, especially to you. Forget it. It's just that . . . well, Elizabeth won't see it either.'

' Is that why you've been having differences of opinion lately?' asked Catherine impulsively, then drew back. ' Oh, I shouldn't have asked that. It's none of my business.'

' Don't apologise. I suppose you'd have to be as blind as a bat not to notice. It's one of the reasons why Elizabeth and I are not exactly seeing eye to eye. Only one of the reasons, though. There are others.'

Again he met her eyes squarely, and she found that her heart was beating more quickly. She didn't want to know what the other reasons were, she told herself. She wasn't ready to know, so she said nothing, concentrating on the well-cooked meal.

' I hope you soon resolve it all,' she said nervously.

' Do you, Catherine?'

' And I would have thought John was very competent.'

' Don't go taking too much interest in John Sheridan,' he told her harshly. ' In any of the Sheridans. They're people out for their own ends.'

' I can't imagine how they could ever make use of me for their own ends. I'm neither brilliantly brainy, nor am I well endowed with worldly goods.'

'I wouldn't be too sure,' he said, very softly.

'I am . . . very sure.'

'Perhaps they're hoping that you'll find something marvellous among all your father's personal papers,' he said, in a teasing voice, though she sensed an odd sort of purpose behind it.

'I'm through with sorting out most of my stuff now, and I'm sorry to disappoint you. And them. I've cleaned out a multitude of old bills, and the only thing of interest was the amount my parents paid for new furniture when they were first married!'

'Do the Sheridans know you've finished now?'

'Of course. Uncle James gives me advice when he can.'

'I'll bet he does!'

Suddenly Catherine felt herself withdraw a little coolly.

'I wish you'd tell me straight what you're hinting, Michael. Did you expect my father to have valuable stocks and shares among his papers? Or did you believe the Sheridans guilty of such a thing?'

'If I said I did, you'd only get mad at me. But just see if their attitude towards you changes at all.'

'But they *couldn't* have thought such an unlikely thing. Uncle James knew Daddy very well. And believe me, if he had any secret source of wealth, Mother would have known.'

'Yes, I suppose she would,' Michael agreed, frowning again.

'You get such odd ideas,' laughed Catherine. Had he overheard some sort of conversation and completely misunderstood it?

'Coffee is being served in the lounge, sir,' the waitress told Michael, and Catherine glanced at her watch as she rose from the table.

'We won't have to be too late, Michael,' she said, rather anxiously.

'Too late? It's early!'

'I know, but Aunt Lucille will wonder where we are. And Elizabeth.'

'All right, we'll go when we've had coffee, though the Sheridans won't be missing us. John probably won't even notice the time.'

'Why?' she asked curiously.

'You may find out, if you're early enough.'

Again it was warm and cosy in the lounge, and Michael began to ask Catherine about freshwater pearls, and to admire the beautiful brooch she always wore, and which was now pinned to her suit.

Animated, she told him all she knew, and he leaned forward, full of interest. The time flew past, and at length she jumped up, startled.

'Michael! We've been here for hours.'

'Don't exaggerate. All right, Cinderella, we'll go now. Haven't you enjoyed my company at all?'

She felt tongue-tied. Part of her had been almost helplessly attracted by his company, like a moth to the light. And part of her was still repelled.

Would she feel the same way if he were free of

Elizabeth? she wondered. But it was difficult to be objective, when Elizabeth was so much part of their lives.

'You're taking your time about answering.'

'I know. I'm sorry. Thank you for bringing me,' she said politely. 'I enjoyed it all very much.'

He had again taken her arm as he escorted her back to the car, then as he slid in beside her and shut the door, he turned to look at her and suddenly pulled her into his arms and kissed her till she struggled.

'That's not fair!' she cried. 'It's not fair to Elizabeth—or to me.'

'Maybe not, though it's fair to me. I've wanted to do that ever since I set eyes on you, and now I have. You bring out the protective instincts in me. And anyway, Elizabeth and I are in limbo . . .'

'But I'm not.'

'Aren't you?'

'You aren't free to talk to me like this.'

'If I were free, Catherine . . . would that make any difference?'

'I doubt it,' she said. 'I'm tired, Michael. I want to go home.'

'Home!' he repeated, then laughed a little. 'All right, I'm sorry. I suppose if you weren't such a hedgehog, you wouldn't be you. You've got standards and that's good. I had standards, too, once. I had them knocked out of me, and I've acquired some all my own.'

He laughed lightly, and she relaxed a little.

'I think you pull my leg, Michael.'

'Perhaps I do.'

They drove the rest of the way in silence, then he pulled up in front of Balgower.

'Here's your case, my dear. Mind if I don't come in? I don't feel like facing the family tonight.'

'Well, of course not. Won't they expect it, though?'

'Why should I have to do what they expect? See you in the morning, Kate. Goodnight.'

'Goodnight,' she echoed, and went up to the front door, letting herself in with her own key.

John met her in the hall, and she turned to smile at him, then saw that he was furiously angry.

'Where have you been, Catherine?' he demanded. 'Your train got in hours ago. Michael promised to bring you straight home.'

Elizabeth was bringing up the rear, looking beyond her to the door.

'Where is he?' she asked.

'He went on home,' said Catherine uncertainly, looking from one to the other. 'We . . . we had something to eat in town.'

'And it's taken you all this time!' cried John. 'Didn't it occur to you we might be worried?'

'Surely I'm old enough to look after myself?' she cried, suddenly angry.

She wasn't used to a family inquisition, and something in Elizabeth's eyes was making her feel

95

uncomfortable.

'Michael said you had friends here,' she said
defensively.

'The Cravens left hours ago,' said John, 'and
Mother and Father have gone to bed.'

'I should like to go to bed, too,' said Catherine
shakily.

It had been an upsetting day in many ways. Saying goodbye to the Neills had really felt like goodbye, now that they were selling the house and
moving to a small one. Catherine had felt as though
her retreat had been cut off. Now it was as though
her future was also far from smooth.

John's anger was beginning to cool.

'I should have known Mike Rodgers would be
behind it,' he said, and Elizabeth's eyes began to
sparkle with anger.

'That's right, blame Michael!' she cried. 'He
probably saw she was tired after the journey, and
gave her a break. And she'd be telling him one
of her great long rambling tales of how good it was
in Scotland when she was a wee girl.'

Catherine coloured furiously, feeling that Elizabeth was sneering at her, then she saw that Elizabeth
was fighting tears, and she nodded rather wearily.

'Got it first time, Elizabeth. That's exactly what
happened. Goodnight, both of you. I'd like to go
straight to bed.'

She mounted the stairs, then went into her bedroom and closed the door, mechanically going

through her toilet before crawling in between the sheets.

It was difficult to decide whether Michael had been more upsetting with his quick kiss, or whether it was Elizabeth with tears sparkling on her lashes.

Or was it John, who looked so different in his anger, his pleasant good-natured face grim and white? The Cravens had left hours ago, he had told her, and the name had stayed in her mind. Rosalie Craven his ex-fiancée. Had she been here, too, and had John's anger and upset stemmed more from seeing her than from her own late arrival?

Or was he merely angry for Elizabeth's sake? Perhaps she was bringing an upsetting influence to the house, thought Catherine, as she lay shivering between the cool smooth sheets. Perhaps she would really have to think again about moving on, hard though it might be.

But to where? And what about money? There would be precious little to tide her over.

Catherine began to feel frightened for her future, and to feel ashamed that she had not a great deal more courage and enterprise. It didn't occur to her that this could have been the result of the accident which changed her life, and that it would take some time before she was her old self again.

She lay, staring at nothing for a long time, then fell into a rather troubled sleep.

CHAPTER VI

Now that Catherine was quite capable of looking after all the pearls, James Sheridan had increased his stock of silverware, fine porcelain and gift items in gold. Elizabeth and Miss Pryce handled all this between them.

Catherine admired the lovely wine goblets, fruit dishes and candelabra, then picked up a small gold pillbox and a cigar cutter, both of which were beautifully made.

'I doubt if I could even afford the swizzle-stick,' she confided to Elizabeth, with a small laugh.

'You'll have to look for a rich husband, then,' said Elizabeth, rather tartly, and Catherine's smile wavered. There was now a small barrier between them, ever since the night Michael had taken her out for dinner.

Catherine wondered, sometimes, whether she ought to clear the air between them, but didn't quite know what to say. Michael was inclined to seek her out whenever he had a free moment, but he was offering to coach her for her F.G.A. examination, and because he was giving her very helpful instructions, Catherine accepted this with gratitude.

Uncle James heartily approved of this, but John viewed it all silently, and Catherine looked at him worried now and again. She found that she was beginning to feel anxious in case she lost John's friendship.

She realised now that he had helped to dispel a lot of her fears and loneliness when she first came, and now they were all tending to crowd back.

' What is the hardness of a ruby on Moe's scale?' Michael asked her.

' Nine.'

' And a sapphire?'

Catherine hesitated, trying to remember.

' Seven . . . I think.'

' No, Catherine. Ruby and sapphire are both corundum. So they are both nine. Do try to remember, and get a bit more homework done. What's the specific gravity of amethyst?'

Catherine did not know, and had to shake her head, her cheeks scarlet, while Elizabeth looked on, speculation in her eyes.

' I . . . I'll have to study a bit more,' she confessed. ' I find it difficult to remember things in my head.'

Michael smiled and gave her hand a warm squeeze.

' All right, my dear. But you need someone behind you to work for, and if the others haven't time, it had better be me. So just remember I'll be asking you about how to test the refrective indices of stones, and I hope you can distinguish between a white zircon and a white spinel, if I suddenly show them both to you one of these days.'

Catherine nodded. She had made good progress at first because she was interested, but now she was finding it all rather difficult, and something seemed to have gone out of the absorbing interest which she had felt for the jewellery in Sheridan and Rodgers. It was probably due to her unsettled stage of mind.

During the morning, after Catherine had carefully polished a pair of diamond and cultured pearl ear-rings and put them into the display case, she looked up to see the loveliest girl she had seen in years walking into the shop. She looked around carefully, then walked over to John with a gay smile.

'John darling, here you are! I did say I might drop in, didn't I?'

Miss Pryce came over to Catherine, and said almost under her breath:

'So she's trying to get her claws into John again, is she? He'll be a fool if he falls for it again.'

Catherine had no need to ask who it was, but she couldn't help it.

'Rosalie Craven?'

'Dear Rosalie! She looks as sweet as pie, but she's been spoiled, that's what. But John got pole-axed the first time he laid eyes on her, and I couldn't possibly guess if it's still the same or not. You can never tell with John. He's very deep.'

Catherine withdrew a little. She did not like to discuss anyone with Miss Pryce, feeling that the older woman was very much inclined to be a gossip. It was almost lunchtime for John, and sometimes he preferred to have coffee and a sandwich in the rooms behind the shop, but today he walked over to have a word with his father and Michael, then he and Rosalie left the shop together, her arm linked companionably in his.

Catherine felt a dullness inside her, and another emotion, which she soon realised was jealousy. She sat down for a moment, taking hold of herself. Surely she couldn't be jealous of this girl who meant so much to John?

Elizabeth had already gone to lunch, and was due back any time. She and Michael sometimes shared lunch break, but Elizabeth had said she had some shopping to do, and Michael had spent part of his lunch break in coaching Catherine.

Now Elizabeth swung through the door, and came straight up to Miss Pryce.

' So Rosalie is on the prowl again,' she remarked. ' She and John have just crossed the street in front of me, and neither of them even noticed me.'

' She hasn't wasted much time,' Miss Pryce remarked.

For a moment Elizabeth stood deliberating, then slowly she hung up her coat.

' Ah, well, back to work, Prycey. I've still got to write out price tickets for those Dresden ornaments, and the Royal Copenhagen.'

' I like this Capo-di-Monte dog,' said Miss Pryce, and for a moment all three women admired the new selection of ornaments, some of them so valuable that Catherine did not feel inclined to handle them.

She turned her attention to tidying up her own items, checking that they were all gently polished and had price tickets, then trying to learn a few facts and figures about diamonds and emeralds before Michael pounced on her again.

She noticed, however, that John and Rosalie were very late back from lunch, and that both looked rather pale. The girl's mouth pouted a little, and she threw a haughty glance in Catherine's direction, then John brought her over to be introduced, his eyes rather intense as they looked at her.

' This is Catherine Lyall, a very old friend and now a member of the family. Catherine, dear . . . Miss Rosalie Craven, also an old friend.'

' How do you do,' Catherine said politely, holding out her hand, which Rosalie barely touched with her slender gloved fingers.

' I rather thought you'd release John from your date with him on Saturday,' she said haughtily. ' We haven't seen each other for ages, and we always go to the Badminton Dance together.' She turned to John, while Catherine began to feel bewildered. ' You know I would love to go again this year, John darling.'

' But it's Catherine's first dance here since she came,' he said smoothly, his eyes meeting hers pleadingly. ' I couldn't possibly ask her to change the arrangements. She's had her new dress for weeks.'

Catherine gathered her wits together, hoping she

was correctly interpreting the looks he was casting at her.

'Well, yes, I'm afraid I did buy something new for the occasion, Miss Craven,' she lied nobly. 'Of course, we had no idea you would be able to go.'

Rosalie ignored her.

'Oh, well, John, I do understand. You won't want to let Miss . . . er . . . the young lady down.'

She smiled sweetly, and went over for a word with Elizabeth, while the smile faded from Catherine's face and she turned rather angrily to John.

'What was all that about?'

'I'll tell you later,' he said, in a low voice.

After he had seen Rosalie out, he came back over to Catherine.

'Thanks, Kate. I don't want to talk about it now, but we can discuss the dance tonight, after we come home. I had intended to ask you, only Rosalie nearly spoiled it. Elizabeth and Michael are going, too.'

'Oh,' she said, and a moment later she was busy with customers who had just come in. But her head was still whirling a little. Had John been making use of her because he did not want to go out with Rosalie Craven for some reason? Or was it true that he had intended to ask her all the time?

Catherine's chin lifted. She wasn't going to be used as an excuse. She would make that very clear to John.

Nevertheless, when John again asked her that evening to go to the dance with him, she agreed rather weakly, and with a sudden surge of excitement again. She really *would* have to buy a new dress as it was ages since she had been to a dance.

'It should be fun. I'd love to come,' she told John, and his eyes lit up.

'That's wonderful, Catherine. I knew you wouldn't let me down.'

'Are you sure you were going to ask me? . . . before Miss Craven came, I mean?' she asked levelly.

'Absolutely sure,' he told her. 'I . . . I'll tell you all about it some time, Kate. It isn't something I want to talk about just yet.'

'All right,' she agreed, and looked at him thoughtfully. Whatever had happened between John and Rosalie Craven had obviously hurt him very much, and was probably still hurting.

Catherine decided to ask Elizabeth to help her choose a dress, but when she sought her out later to ask her advice, she overheard her still talking shop to John.

'Have you seen this new shop called Newclox, John?'

'No, I can't say I have. Why, Liz? What's on your mind?'

Elizabeth deliberated, then sighed deeply.

'I don't know. But something about it worries me, John. And I'm sure they get a lot of our trade.'

'Perhaps they sell cheaper clocks with a bigger turnover. Anyway, it's fair competition, surely.'

'So long as it *is* fair.'

'How could it not be?'

She turned away as Catherine walked forward.

'I don't know. Maybe it's just me. Sorry, my dear, forget it. Hello, Catherine. All out to enjoy yourself on Saturday?'

'I hope so. I . . . I was wondering if you could help me . . . choose a dress, I mean. You've got such good taste, Elizabeth.'

The older girl stood still and considered her, then she gave a short laugh.

'All right, my dear, I'll help you. I'll make you the belle of the ball, as they say. It might be . . . rather fun.'

Elizabeth went into her bedroom and shut the door. It hadn't sounded as though it would be much fun, and Catherine turned away, even more perplexed. Why was Elizabeth behaving like this? Surely she couldn't still be jealous of her. After all, she was going with John, not with Michael.

She made her way slowly downstairs, where Aunt Lucille pounded on her as a sympathetic ear into which she could pour her news items of the day.

With a small sigh, Catherine settled down to listen.

The dress which Elizabeth helped Catherine to choose was the loveliest she had ever owned. The older girl had studied her thoughtfully, her long slender fingers drumming on the dressing table, after coming to her room that night.

'You need a hair-do, and a hairdresser who knows when to leave well alone. I'll make an appointment for you. Also you're inclined to put on a little too much make-up at the moment.'

Catherine flushed. It was true. In Perth she had scarcely used make-up at all, but now she used it as a sort of defence, as though hiding her real face from the world.

'It never really spoils what is underneath,' Elizabeth said, rather more gently. 'I doubt if you could do that if you tried.'

Catherine said nothing, and again Elizabeth considered her.

'You're a strange girl,' she said at length, sitting down on the bed. 'You've been given your beauty, yet sometimes I think you couldn't care less. You comb your hair at top speed each morning, slap on make-up, then you hardly look at yourself for the rest of the day, apart from washing off the grime. You treat your complexion shamefully, yet it still stays fresh for you.'

'I . . . I forget,' Catherine excused herself.

'Exactly. You forget.' Elizabeth sighed and heaved herself off the bed. 'We'll go shopping to-morrow lunch-time, and buy you a stunning dress. I think I know where to find it. Something simple and sweet, rather than smart. You can outshine any dress, Kate, so we'll concentrate on showing you off, rather than the dress.'

'I'm grateful, Elizabeth,' she said gravely. 'Only I . . . I can't afford high prices.'

'No more can I,' said Elizabeth, with a short laugh. 'Don't worry, we can surely find something which won't leave you skint.'

Catherine chuckled, and Elizabeth's rather austere face broke into a smile.

'You've been nice to me ever since I was practically foisted on to you,' said Catherine impulsively. 'I've wanted to thank you for it many times. I . . . I would never do anything to hurt you in return.'

'Sometimes one has only to be oneself, to hurt other people,' Elizabeth told her, then she walked the few paces to the door. 'Don't worry, Catherine. It's suited us very well, having you here. You've come to us at the best possible time. It's we who should be grateful to you.'

She closed the door gently, and Catherine prepared for bed, though it was some time before she fell asleep.

The dress which Elizabeth chose for her next day was of cream silk, simply cut. Her dark hair, still long but beautifully cut, gleamed with brushing, and with Elizabeth's help, her skin glowed like a pearl, which was how John described her later in the evening.

Catherine knew she looked her best as she walked downstairs with Elizabeth, who was herself looking smart and elegant in a gold sheath dress. She had taken pride in Catherine's beauty, and smiled when her mother and father exclaimed when they saw her.

'My dear, you look lovely!' said Lucille.

'It was all Elizabeth's doing.'

'Very nice,' agreed Uncle James, and John stopped in the doorway as he entered the room. He made no comment, but for a moment something glowed in his eyes.

'Don't you think she looks nice?' asked Lucille.

'Very nice,' he echoed. 'Are you coming with us, Elizabeth, or do you prefer to use your new car? Or, of course, is Michael coming for you?'

Elizabeth looked even more cool than ever.

'He offered to come, but I thought it more sensible if I go with you.'

'Come on, then,' said John. 'Time we went.'

He was looking very tall and elegant in his dark clothes, and Catherine couldn't help feeling a tiny bit disappointed that he had not shown more interest in her dress. Some of the free and easy comradeship had gone out of her relationship with John and her mind sought for what had gone wrong. She could only think of Rosalie Craven. Perhaps he was feeling unhappy over Rosalie, and although the girl seemed to want to pick up the threads again, for some reason, perhaps John was afraid of being hurt all over again.

Catherine sighed. She knew too little of what had gone before to judge.

'Are you warm enough?' asked John, adjusting the car heater as she pulled the small fur jacket Aunt Lucille had lent her closer to her neck.

'Oh, yes, thanks.'

Her sudden shiver had had nothing to do with the cold.

'We'll soon be there,' said Elizabeth. 'Oh . . . I might not be coming back with you two. I may want to leave early.'

'No doubt Michael will bring you home,' said John, rather dryly, and his sister didn't reply.

Michael was waiting for them in the foyer of the hotel, and he stepped forward, looking immaculate in his dark suit, though his clothes were very much more modern than John's.

There was no doubt that he was a very handsome young man, thought Catherine, when she caught sight of him, and his gaze on her was intense before Elizabeth stepped forward and took his arm.

'I hope you haven't been kept waiting, darling,' she said sweetly, and Michael murmured something which Catherine couldn't catch.

It was a strange mixed-up evening, from her point of view. As John escorted her through to the dance floor, after leaving her jacket in the cloakroom, she gave herself up to the enjoyment of dancing again. For a moment her thoughts were on Philip, as John was the first man with whom she had danced since she used to go regularly with Philip.

But she could now think of him with gentleness

and not the searing pain of loss, and she felt that he would be happy to see her here, among other young people, learning to enjoy her life again.

John was an excellent dancer, and as Catherine looked up at him she began to see that there was strength and purpose on his face which was lacking in Michael's, whose good looks were often rather sulky. She had always thought of the other man as much the better-looking of the two, but now she was wondering why she had ever believed such a thing. With his older, more traditional clothes, John looked far more distinguished.

' Do you really like my dress?' she asked shyly.

He'd had so little to say to her that she felt almost tongue-tied. His face relaxed a little.

' You look like a pearl,' he told her, and her cheeks glowed a little with colour.

' That's quite a compliment. You know how much I love and admire pearls.'

' Then you must consider yourself "of great price",' he told her gravely.

Michael claimed her for the next dance, holding her very close so that she tried to break free a little.

' I'm sorry, but I can't dance like that,' she told him, watching John sweep past with Elizabeth. She felt embarrassed with Michael gazing down into her face.

' Why should we have an old-fashioned waltz if I can't hold you close? You're looking very lovely, Catherine.'

'Elizabeth chose everything for me,' she said deliberately. 'She helped me buy my dress, and have my hair cut properly.'

'She has very good taste,' he told her smoothly, 'but you are still lovely. However, I rather think someone is trying to outdo you.'

She looked in the direction he had indicated, and saw that Rosalie Craven, in a stunning white and silver crêpe dress which showed her beautiful arms and shoulders to perfection, had just come in, accompanied by a young man with a rather loud laugh, which sounded even above the music as they stood talking at the door.

'She'll be making a beeline for our John,' said Michael, his eyes gleaming into hers. 'She gave him the go-by when an American family came over on holiday, and she got friendly with the son. They were decidedly rich, and I rather think she thought herself all set for marriage, and a nice easy life in America, with all the trimmings. But now she's home again, minus any sort of ring—even John's little flowery one.'

'That's a lovely ring!' cried Catherine. 'I'm sure any girl would be proud to wear it.'

'Are you getting cross?' asked Michael. 'Would *you* be thinking that it might fit you? If so, you might save yourself a lot of heartache by forgetting all about it.'

'I think my feelings are my own affair, Michael,' said Catherine, and already she could feel a sudden ache in her heart. Already Rosalie Craven was making straight for John, and all four were standing together in a small group.

'I suppose we'd better go and join them,' said Michael, with resignation, and at his suggestion they all sat down round one of the tables, and John ordered refreshments. After the first initial stare Rosalie chose to ignore Catherine, though her friend, Dick Curzon, was only too happy to include her in the conversation. He was a cheerful young man, and Catherine found herself responding to his easy chatter. It was refreshing to find someone who did not seem to have a lot on their mind!

John was looking rather grim, and Elizabeth wore her rather haughty look, though Michael and Rosalie were beginning to sparkle. Rosalie was telling them of a wonderful evening she had spent in America, and Michael was obviously enjoying hearing all about it.

'You've promised me the next dance, John darling,' she said, as the music changed, and without a word he rose and lifted back her chair, as she stood up.

'Shall we try this one?' asked Dicky Curzon, and Catherine nodded and smiled. As she left the table, she saw that Elizabeth had leaned forward to talk to Michael, and that they seemed to be arguing a little.

Dicky danced well, and Catherine tried to enjoy it all more, though she couldn't help a twinge of jealousy when she saw how well John and Rosalie Craven danced together.

Soon, however, John came to claim her again, though it seemed to her that there was even more restraint between them.

'Er . . . if you want to dance with Miss Craven, please don't worry about me,' she told him, and he glowered at her.

'You're my partner, Catherine. I shall dance with you.'

'But . . .'

'You mean you object? You'd rather dance with someone else? Mike Rodgers, for instance?'

She flushed deeply at his tone.

'Why should you object to that, if Elizabeth doesn't?'

'What makes you think she doesn't?'

She looked over and saw that they had gone from the table, but she could not see them on the dance floor.

'I'm afraid you'll have to put up with me,' John told her, and she flushed.

'Surely I don't have to put up with anyone!'

He sighed.

'That's true. I'm sorry, Catherine, I've got rather a headache. Do you mind if we leave rather early, my dear?'

'Why, no, of course not.'

Was he running away? From Rosalie?

They stayed for two more dances, then Catherine

collected her jacket, and John took her out into the clear, rather frosty evening and helped her into the car. He drove silently, and it was a moment or two before Catherine realised they weren't on their way home.

'This surely isn't the way, John.'

'No, I thought I'd drive for a little. I like to look at the countryside by moonlight. The trees are enchanting. Do you mind, Catherine? Are you warm enough?'

'Yes, I'm warm enough, and I don't mind.'

She snuggled down into the car, and they drove in silence for some way along winding country roads until it seemed that John had exhausted the black mood into which he had fallen. Finally he pulled up at a lay-by beside a small stream, which sparkled in the moonlight, and murmured rhythmically as it flowed past.

Catherine felt her heart begin to beat rather fast as John turned to look at her, then a moment later she was in his arms, and he was kissing her fiercely.

'It's time someone did that, and it had better be me,' he told her, and she pulled away angrily.

'What do you mean, John? I'm not asking anyone to make love to me.'

'Aren't you?'

'Don't make me mad at you, John. If you're annoyed with Miss Craven, don't take it out on me!'

'I'm not annoyed with Miss Craven. Oh, for goodness' sake, Kate, don't let's end the evening with a quarrel. I . . . I wanted it to be very different. As a matter of fact, I wanted to . . . to ask you to marry me.'

She gasped. It was the last thing she expected. 'You can't be serious!'

'I'm not in the habit of making proposals unless I am serious.'

He hadn't said he loved her. Catherine wanted to ask, but a strange inner shyness kept stopping her. 'Why?' she managed at last. 'Why ask me?'

'Because I want you, silly girl. And I need you, Catherine. If you married me, it would solve quite a lot of problems.'

It would keep him clear of Rosalie, she thought. Was he using her as a shield against the other girl, as he had done when he asked her to the dance? The girl obviously disturbed him, and Catherine could not be sure that she wasn't being offered second best.

Then, too, did John think Michael was paying her too much attention? Did he think that Elizabeth would be happier if she became engaged to John?

Catherine said nothing, though misery was gathering in her heart. If only he had told her he had fallen in love with her, and wanted to marry her for her own sake!

'I . . . I don't know,' she managed at last, because truly she did not know. Her head seemed to be whirling, and her emotions so mixed that part of her wanted to go into John's arms again, and feel safe for always, yet another part of her was afraid.

She might lose it all again if he was only asking her impulsively, and she could not bear any more losses.

'I'm sorry, Catherine,' he apologised. 'I've gone blundering in when I should be remembering that you've got a lot to forget. I hope you can forget this, too, my dear. It never happened.'

Swiftly he started the car engine again, and in silence they drove back home. She felt confused and dissatisfied, sitting there in the luxury of her lovely new dress and Aunt Lucille's fur jacket.

It seemed that something precious was gradually slipping through her fingers, as the street lights began to grow brighter, and they made for the quiet suburbs.

'Should we talk about it again, John?' she asked in a small voice as he stopped the car at the front door, and for a long moment he sat still, then turned to look into her face by the light which shone above the front door.

Then he sighed.

'No, my dear, I think we ought to leave it. We're all a little upset . . . hardly the proper atmosphere for a lasting engagement.' He kissed her very gently. 'You're tired, so bed for you after a hot drink.'

Catherine's throat felt tight with tears. She had wanted to talk again, but it was obvious that John didn't. Perhaps he had only asked her impulsively, after all.

Her chin lifted, and she managed to smile and

laugh lightly.

'All right, John dear. I guess I have been a little lonely . . . after Philip . . . just as I'm sure you're lonely, too. Goodnight. See you tomorrow.'

He nodded, his eyes bleak, then turned away, and Catherine went straight up to bed. She wondered if Elizabeth was in, and caught faint muffled sounds coming from her room.

If she hadn't known Elizabeth better, she would have wondered if she was crying.

CHAPTER VII

Spring was full upon them and Miss Pryce prophesied
a spate of engagement ring buyers. Catherine had
seen several young couples peering in the window
and comparing settings and costs.

'Sometimes I think we sell far more wedding rings
than engagement rings,' said Miss Pryce, with a
sigh. 'Young couples seem to make up their minds
so quickly these days, then they just go off and get
married.'

'Not all of us,' protested Catherine. 'I was
engaged for a year before . . .' She broke off,
then continued with a small sigh: 'Before my wedding was arranged.'

'I'm sorry, my dear,' Miss Pryce apologised. 'I
forgot.'

Since she had taken to avoiding Michael Rodgers,
Miss Pryce had been very nice to her. Catherine
wondered if it had all been her imagination, but she
now realised that Miss Pryce admired both Elizabeth
and Michael, and only wanted their happiness.

'I'm over it now,' she assured the older woman.
'It's like something that happened in another world.'

Her eyes had almost unconsciously gone to John,
who was making out a list of rings whose sizes had
to be altered to suit the customers who had already
bought them.

'Miss Craven seems determined to share her lunch hour with John,' said Miss Pryce darkly. 'She's been in twice this week already. And always with an excuse—a small chain for her friend's little girl, or someone else's watch to be repaired. She's determined to get back on the old footing.'

Catherine nodded. John had treated her with his old gentleness and good humour ever since the night of the dance. It was as though his proposal had never happened, and Catherine tried to pretend to herself that it didn't matter. But she kept remembering every detail more and more, and wishing she had not been so taken aback. She might have given a very different answer.

Yet what was the use of that? It had been an impulsive proposal, and John would only have regretted it later.

Michael, too, was holding himself rather aloof since the dance, his eyes thoughtful as he busied himself with his own work. He left for an early lunch that day, saying he had a man to meet at a club nearby, then came back accompanied by a tall man in a well-cut suit and a bright tie with a matching shirt.

'The diamonds are this way,' he was saying. 'Mr John Sheridan will help you, I'm sure.'

John smiled at the newcomer, and Michael quickly hurried away saying he had to attend to something urgently. Catherine saw the man examining some beautiful diamond brooches with earrings to match, then it was her turn to go to lunch.

Three days later she wished heartily that she had paid more attention to the purchaser, when Uncle James called both John and Michael into the office, and the storm which Catherine had sensed for a long time began to break.

'Who made the sale?' James Sheridan demanded. 'Our finest diamond brooch and matching earrings!'

'I did,' John told him.

'And accepted a cheque. You must know we only accept cheques in certain circumstances. In other words, if we can be sure they won't bounce!'

John went pale. 'Has it?'

'Yes.'

He glanced at Michael.

'But . . . but I don't understand. The man was managing director of Newcomer's, the wine importers. You remember, Mike? I . . . I asked you and you said he was absolutely O.K.'

'I said the firm was O.K.,' corrected Michael, his eyes gleaming a little. 'I know nothing about the man, John. . . .'

'You brought him up to my counter!'

'I'd only just met him at the door,' said Michael. 'You aren't shifting the blame to my doorstep.'

John's face had gone white and hard as he looked back at his father.

'Then it looks as though I'm entirely to blame,' he said harshly. 'One of the oldest tricks in the book, and I fell for it. It . . . it was quite a sale, too.'

He looked again at the returned cheque, then stared at his father. There was no disguising that the loss was very serious.

'You didn't think of checking?' asked James Sheridan quietly.

'Hell, no! I thought he was someone Mike knew and when he offered a cheque, I asked Mike if it was O.K., and he said it was. . . .'

'The *firm* was,' corrected Michael. 'How did I know you hadn't checked him out?'

John said nothing. The responsibility was his.

'Leave us, Michael,' said James Sheridan heavily, and Michael went out and shut the door.

Catherine's stand was closest to the office and it was difficult for her not to overhear when voices were raised. She had not been busy, and she found herself becoming involved in the argument. Michael *had* escorted the man to John's counter. It *had* appeared as though he had known him. Surely John wasn't entirely to blame.

She looked up as Michael left the office and came over to her.

'You heard?'

'How could I help it? I've told Uncle James before that if he raises his voice, I can hear. I'm afraid you all forgot.'

'I suppose we did. Fancy old John falling for that one. And what a sum! There's going to be changes, I'll bet. The firm can't afford a loss like that, and no insurance will pay up for carelessness. I knew that, given time, he would have us ruined.'

'That's not fair!' cried Catherine hotly. 'You ought to take half the blame. You must have realised John would think you knew the man.'

Michael regarded her thoughtfully.

'He's got a good defender in you, Catherine,' he said at last. 'Don't tell me you're beginning to . . . to care for John. That would be a laugh!'

'Why should it?'

He looked down at her.

'I thought you had more sense,' he told her, quietly, 'and that you'd tumble to it long before now.'

'Tumble to what?'

'The Sheridans. They hang on to people till it suits them. Then they get rid of them when it doesn't.'

'You've experience of this?' she asked, her eyes challenging.

'Yes. My father. James Sheridan soon got rid of him when it suited him. . . .'

The office door opened and James and John came out. John glanced at Michael and Catherine talking together, then he went over to attend to his own work without a word.

Catherine saw a customer coming forward to look at pearls, and was grateful to have something to do. Was there any truth in what Michael had said? But, if there was, why had he got engaged to

Elizabeth?

Her mind pondered the problem, even as she lifted out double and triple strings of creamy-white pearls to be admired. Could it be that he was pulling away from Elizabeth after he discovered that they did use other people, and that was the reason for the strain on their relationship?

If he broke away from them, it would have to be a complete break. He would have to start afresh as an employee in another firm, and perhaps there would be difficulties in leaving Uncle James. Perhaps the Sheridans could not afford to buy Michael out of the partnership. Was this why Catherine could often sense trouble, and why Michael complained so loudly that John was making mistakes?

But surely he could have done more to prevent this loss. Catherine's eyes were troubled, though she smiled at her customer as she chose a single string of graduated pearls, and she reached for one of the lovely presentation boxes in which to lay the pearls.

As she wrapped them carefully, she could see that Elizabeth, who was having a late lunch, had only just come in, and had just heard about the bounced cheque. She had gone over for a word with Michael.

' I want to talk to you tonight,' she said quietly. ' We could go in my car to the usual place.'

' Oh . . . all right, though this is usually the night you help your mother with one of her charities.'

' Catherine can take my place. This is important,

Michael.'

'O.K., Liz darling. No need to get the gun out.'

Catherine saw her flush and turn away, then come over to her.

'Can you help Mother with those ladies who come on Thursdays? You know . . . tea and cakes handed round, and take notes for her. She always gets mixed up if you don't.'

'Of course,' she agreed.

'Bless you, Catherine.'

There was a small catch in Elizabeth's voice, but as she walked away, she seemed her usual composed self, and Catherine shrugged a little. There was surely enough trouble without her imagining more.

That evening John took her home, a silent John who seemed to have gone cold and hard.

'You heard what happened?' he asked Catherine flatly.

'Yes. I couldn't help overhearing. John . . . I don't think you were to blame. It . . . it was just an unfortunate misunderstanding.'

'Thanks for the loyalty,' he said dryly, 'but it's misplaced. No, I'm to blame all right. I should never have accepted the man merely because he was someone Mike Rodgers knew, and could vouch for.'

'But Michael didn't know him.'

There was silence for a moment.

'No, he didn't, did he?' John's voice was oddly strained. 'I rather think I'm going to be busy over the next week or two.'

'Doing what?' she asked.

'Recovering the money . . . somehow.'

'Do you think you could find the man again, and get your money back?'

'Confidence men aren't so easy to find. Well, here we are, home again.'

'And I must see Aunt Lucille,' Catherine told him. 'It's my turn to help her tonight. Elizabeth is going out with Michael.'

For a moment John sat very still, then he gave a short laugh and opened the car door.

'Good luck to her, Kate. When Mother holds her committee meetings, I make myself scarce. They change their minds so often, I wouldn't know where I was among them all. Still, that might be better than complete loyalty to one purpose . . . if it's misplaced.'

He took her arm as he escorted her into the house and she could feel the steely grip of his fingers. Catherine wanted to slip her hand into his, and to tell him that she would always be there, if he needed to talk to her.

Then Rosalie Craven came sailing out of the drawing room towards them, and came over to kiss John's cheek, ignoring Catherine but for a brief nod.

'Darling, I forgot to tell you. Mother insisted that I ask you to dinner tonight, and I thought I had. Only Lucille says I didn't, when I rang to check. It's going to make things difficult if you don't come, as Mother has invited the Eastons and

Leon and Helen Cartwright, so please, can you come? We'll go in my car if you're tired.'

John was obviously tired, but after a while he nodded.

' Maybe I could do with a break tonight, Rosalie,' he agreed. ' I have to get things in perspective. I must thank Mrs Craven for the invitation. Oh, and I'll take my own car for the sake of getting home.'

' But, darling, *I* can bring you home. . . .'

Catherine didn't wait to hear the reply. Quickly she ran upstairs to wash and change for Aunt Lucille's committee meeting.

When she came down for tea, she found it a silent meal, with only Uncle James, Aunt Lucille and herself. Obviously the older woman had been told about the cheque, and even she was subdued.

What would happen now? wondered Catherine. Would the firm really have to cut down? And if they could no longer afford many staff, who would have to go?

Her own salary was not too large, but it would amount to quite a lot over a year. And they couldn't ask Miss Pryce to go. Not after so many years. The others were all members of the family, and Mike a partner.

Again Catherine began to look into the future. As though in answer to her thoughts, Uncle James's quiet voice penetrated her mind.

' Have you tidied all your papers now, Catherine?'

' Just one more small box, Uncle James. I'll

finish it on Saturday. It's taken age
so much to go through, and . . .
concentrate all the time.'

He smiled kindly.

' I know, my dear. When you
Saturday, come to my study, and v
about investments. I think you oug
return possible for the little your f

She nodded. It was only a few
wouldn't want her to invest it in the
he? Uncomfortably she remember
ing her that Uncle James used peo
had used his father. How could he
if they were partners? Wouldn't t
thing?

' Uncle James, was Michael's
partner? I mean, did he do a lot t
its feet?'

A shutter seemed to come over J
face as Catherine asked the question. He stared at
her, his eyes burning, and Aunt Lucille pushed back
her chair a little.

' Frederick Rodgers has been dead for ten years,'
he said, rather harshly. ' I don't think we can discuss him now, and his effect on the firm. Who has
been telling you about him, Catherine? Michael?'

' He . . . he only said he had been a partner. I
wondered what . . . what it had been like in those
days.'

' Oh.' James Sheridan folded his napkin carefully, and slid it into an antique silver ring. 'Michael was little more than a schoolboy when his father died. His mother has married again. I rather think he prefers to remember and love his own father, rather than his stepfather, even if he likes and respects him, too. Very understandable. Though he's taking a long time to settle down to life. He's very restless. Perhaps marriage to Elizabeth will help. He needs a steadying influence.'

'He certainly doesn't need me,' said a voice from the doorway, and Elizabeth walked into the room, her face deathly pale, and her eyes glittering brightly.

'Elizabeth darling! Catherine said you were going out . . . you and Michael. . . .'

'Only to talk over something. It didn't take long. I'm no longer engaged to Michael. I've given him back his ring.'

'Darling!' cried her mother again. 'But you and he . . . you and he . . . it's been understood for years. . . .'

'I won't be married off because it's so suitable!' cried Elizabeth.

'But I thought you loved him!' cried Lucille, and Catherine felt her heart go out to the other girl, as her strong composure suddenly gave way, and Elizabeth was just another young girl sobbing her heart out, while her father went round to hold her in his arms.

'He's . . . he's been blaming John for . . . for making mistakes and losing us money. Only *he's* the one who's been behind it all. He definitely told John that the cheque was O.K. I *heard* him. I *heard* him, I tell you! He says he meant the firm, but he told John the man was O.K., knowing that John would think he was a friend from his club, bringing him in as he did. Mike knows heaps of people from his club, and knows a great deal about what's going on. I tell you, he knew all about that man, even if he denies it.'

Elizabeth had stopped crying.

' And he kept encouraging people to go elsewhere. I could see it all happening, and when I tried to talk to him, he kept putting me off, and pretending it was I who was jealous of Catherine.'

Here Elizabeth's composure broke again.

' I tried to show it didn't matter and I didn't care, for Catherine's sake. I didn't want her to become involved. And I hoped she would ignore it when Mike started looking at her so . . . so deliberately, and blaming what I had to say on jealousy. I . . . I think John sensed it, too, and got angry.'

Elizabeth sobbed quietly for a few moments and James Sheridan stood up, his face white.

' Young rascal,' he said at length. ' That's the finish. Tomorrow he starts to look for another job.'

' I don't know what's happened to him,' said Elizabeth. ' I really thought he cared for me . . . as . . . as I cared for him. . . .'

After a while she became a little calmer, and more like the old Elizabeth.

'Your friends will soon be arriving, Mother,' she said, wiping her eyes. 'Can you help, Catherine?'

'Of course,' she said readily. 'I . . . I'm sorry, Elizabeth.'

'No need to worry,' said Elizabeth, with a watery smile. 'I'll get over it. It happens all the time, but we survive.'

She excused herself and went upstairs, and Aunt Lucille took Catherine's arm as they went into the lounge, where, shortly, her ladies arrived and she got involved in a great deal of chatter, even if only Catherine knew what an effort she was making to keep it a normal evening.

Catherine's thoughts turned to Michael. So it was Michael who would be leaving the firm! Uncle James had spoken as though he were an employee, though, not a partner. That seemed strange, but it was not really her affair. That could all be left to Uncle James.

Yet it would be strange without Michael in the shop. She thought of his dark good looks, and of the strange disturbing effect he'd had on her when she first came. That was when he was deliberately taking notice of her.

Would the restless, disturbing atmosphere she had often experienced about the shop disappear after Michael went?

No one ever knew what James Sheridan said to Michael Rodgers. This time the office door was firmly closed, and when Michael appeared, his face was very white and he walked over to collect a few of his personal things, then made for the door, pausing only to look for a long moment at Elizabeth.

Catherine felt her heart shake as she watched, aware of some sort of intense feeling between them, then Michael was gone, and Elizabeth standing rigid and composed.

Miss Pryce seemed to be the most affected, her face scarlet as she buzzed about like an angry bee.

'They'll be sorry,' she muttered to Catherine. 'It was Michael's right to be here. His father helped to build all this. It is his son's right to take his place here with the others.'

'Only if he gives complete loyalty,' Catherine said, rather absently, looking at John, who had just come in.

'Michael has gone,' Miss Pryce told him loudly. 'Your father has just fired him.'

John said nothing, but strode on into the office. He had been home late the previous evening, and had been told the main details of what had happened. Now they could hear low voices as he talked things over with his father, and when he appeared, his face was cold and inscrutable.

'My father and I will take care of the clocks and watches till Mr . . . Mr Rodgers is replaced,' he said flatly, and Miss Pryce sniffed. John looked at her levelly, and she flushed.

'Yes, Miss Pryce?' he asked quietly.

'Nothing. I didn't speak . . . er . . . Mr John.'

He continued to gaze at her for a moment, and Catherine felt that a change had been made indeed, and that John's presence was now going to be felt very much more. She looked at him, trying to remember the evening he had kissed her and asked her to marry him. But he seemed an entirely different person.

Soon, however, they were all kept busy with Michael being away, and a new routine was established. But although he was no longer in the shop, it was as though his disturbing presence hung over all of them.

Elizabeth still loved him, thought Catherine, looking at the other girl's pale face and shadowed eyes, and it had cost Uncle James a big effort of will to break things off with Michael. Had it also cost him money he could ill afford at the moment? wondered Catherine.

Nor did John look any happier for having Michael removed. Most of the extra work was falling on his shoulders, and later he remarked to his father that reorganisation might help a little. Perhaps he had really liked Michael, thought Catherine, looking at his rather harassed face. Certainly he was far from elated now that the other man had gone, even though he had often taken all the blame for mistakes which ought to have been shared.

And Catherine? She, too, felt a gap had been made, and kept remembering how he had helped her with her studies in gemmology. She had not thanked him enough, she thought, rather forlornly.

Now it was unlikely that she would ever see him again.

CHAPTER VIII

The following Sunday John came down to breakfast, looking a little brighter and happier. It was another beautiful day, with more warmth in the sun. Already the hedgerows were budding, with tiny green leaves, and everywhere fresh daffodils and crocuses swayed gently in the breeze.

'I love this time of year,' said Catherine, looking out at the garden. 'It always brings one a little bit of hope for the future. I mean, everything seems to burst with life, after the dullness of winter.'

'I know exactly what you mean,' said John, coming to stand beside her, 'though life really is going on all the time, even if it does seem dormant now and again. The jasmine on the side wall flowered all winter, and didn't you see the aconites and all those snowdrops up in the shrubbery?'

'Of course I did,' she smiled, 'but the trees were still rather dead-looking, and now they're alive again. Lambs are being born and the birds are nesting. Everything surges with life. Don't you feel it, John?'

He looked at her strangely.

'Yes, I feel it.'

'Feel what?' asked Elizabeth, appearing at the door. She was very thin, thought Catherine, suddenly seeing Elizabeth in a beam of sunlight, and feeling a pang of anxiety for her. She knew that Lucille was also concerned for her daughter, and had wanted Elizabeth to take an early holiday.

'Somewhere warm and relaxing, darling,' she had coaxed.

'Sounds like bed,' said Elizabeth, with a small laugh. 'No, dear, you know I can't go helping myself to time off now that . . . while we're short-staffed. I'll have my holiday in July, as I've arranged.'

'You don't eat enough.'

'Of course I do. I'm naturally skinny. I'd have no clothes if I put on any weight.'

Now Catherine could see why Lucille was concerned. Elizabeth was normally very thin and willowy, but now she looked frail, her slender hands almost transparent.

'What do you feel?' she was asking.

'That it's a gorgeous day,' said John, 'and I think we ought to go somewhere and enjoy it. How about it, Catherine? Like to go to the seaside? Or in-country?'

She hesitated. 'If Elizabeth comes, too.'

'Oh, no, my love, you don't get Elizabeth to go joy-riding today,' the other girl told her. 'The garden and our old hammock is good enough for me.'

Catherine's eyes met John's, and she could sense the concern in him.

'A good run in the fresh air and a hamper of

goodies might be just the thing you need, Liz,' he told her seriously. ' You're a bit nervy these days.'

She flushed.

' If you mean I'm still trying to get over Michael,' she said deliberately, ' then you're right. I am. But I have to fight my battles in my own way, and you two would just get on my nerves with your sympathy, and your efforts at stuffing food down my throat. If you want to be kind, then leave me alone. I shan't mope, don't worry.'

' All right, hinny,' said John gently, and Catherine saw a sudden flash of tears in Elizabeth's eyes.

' Go on, both of you,' she insisted.

' All right, give us time,' laughed John. ' We haven't got our coffee and sandwiches made yet . . . or should we chance it, and plump for somewhere we can be sure of getting lunch?'

' No, I'd like a picnic,' Catherine decided. ' I'll make it.'

' Good girl,' John approved. ' I'll change my shoes and get the car out.'

' Don't forget that Rosalie is coming to dinner this evening,' said Elizabeth sweetly, and John's face darkened.

' I hadn't forgotten,' he said briefly.

' You'll be back in time?'

' Of course.'

Catherine felt that the sun shone less brightly. Rosalie was becoming a regular visitor to the house, and it was difficult to know whether John welcomed her, or not. Sometimes she caught his eyes lingering on the girl with intensity, and she didn't blame him. Rosalie had more than mere beauty. She was a very dominant personality, and Catherine could guess that it would be hard to resist her when she was being charming.

As far as she was concerned, Rosalie had learned to acknowledge her presence, though they weren't exactly the best of friends. In fact, Catherine often felt that the other girl really disliked her.

'Well, where shall we go?' asked John, when she was ready, having changed into dark blue slacks and a colourful tunic, with her anorak over her arm in case the weather became mischievous and swapped the warm sunshine for biting winds.

'Would you prefer the coast . . . Whitley Bay, South Shields, Seahouses, Bamburgh . . . or would you prefer to go the other way to the North Tyne Valley?'

'Bamburgh,' said Catherine, after a pause. 'I want to look at Bamburgh Castle. It's supposed to be . . .' She paused. She had been going to say very romantic, but changed her mind. '. . . be very historic, isn't it?'

'Very,' agreed John, with a sideways grin, 'but I expect you've also heard that it's supposed to be to where Sir Lancelot eloped with Queen Guinevere, so it's very romantic, too.'

The ready colour stole into her cheeks.

'I rather think King Arthur's court spread itself all over the country,' she said dryly. 'He lived in Scotland, Wales, Cornwall, Bath, and now Northumberland!'

'Romance gets around,' John told her gravely. 'It's got a habit of popping up all over the country.'

'Like spring,' agreed Catherine, changing the subject. 'Oh, look, John, just look at those tiny lambs! Oh, there are two black ones!'

'You get black sheep everywhere, too.'

'Yes,' agreed Catherine, suddenly sobered.

She sat quietly beside him till they reached the pretty town of Alnwick, where a break for coffee soon had her in good spirits again, and working up an appetite for lunch as soon as they reached Bamburgh.

They sat on the grass above the lashing sea, with a breeze now blowing up. Catherine found the small place utterly charming, and got her fill of the old coastal stronghold which was Bamburgh Castle.

John became his old companionable self, and the time seemed to fly past as they walked through the small town hand in hand, and the sea air blew Catherine's dark hair into her eyes, while John laughingly pulled it back so that he could see her face.

'You're happier now, aren't you, Kate?' he asked, gazing into her face. 'The shadows are all going.'

She nodded. 'All the old shadows are going. But

I often think we always get new ones to take their place.'

He was silent, taking his hand from her cheek, and walking beside her with both hands thrust into his pockets.

'Have you felt the shadows . . . since Michael went?' he asked bluntly, and she thought again of Elizabeth's pale face and slender white hands.

'Yes,' she agreed. 'Things haven't been . . . quite the same.'

He said nothing, but kicked at a stone, then looked at his watch.

'Oh, lord, look at the time! We'd better be getting back, Kate. The Cravens are coming, and we've got to get changed before dinner or Mother will be all in a flap. Want to see anything more before we leave?'

'No.'

She shook her head. The lovely day was over. Just for a moment, as they drove down the charming narrow country roads, there had been no shadows, only sunshine, but now she was going back to sit at the dinner table and watch another girl laughing up into John's face, and reminding him of the happy days they had spent in each other's company, days no doubt even brighter and happier for John than today.

Often she had imagined a younger John happily designing the pretty little flowered ring set in diamonds and emeralds, now no doubt being worn by some other girl. Had John regretted the sudden anger which had made him put it into his showcase and sell it again? Had he been hurt that Rosalie did not want it, not even as a keepsake, when their engagement was at an end?

Perhaps she regretted that now, and would be glad to wear the little ring all over again. But it had been wrong for her, decided Catherine, agreeing with Miss Pryce. Rosalie would only want diamonds, and the bigger, the better.

' You're very quiet,' said John at her side, as he drove carefully back home, the fine weather having tempted many cars out on to the roads.

' I find it difficult to talk for the sake of talking,' she said clearly.

' That's supposed to be admirable in a woman.'

' And in a man, I would have thought.'

' Have you had a happy day?'

' Yes, thanks.'

' That's good. I . . . want you to be happy, Catherine.'

' Don't start feeling responsible for me,' she said, rather tartly, and he glanced at her, then concentrated on driving through traffic till he turned off at Balgower.

' Give me the basket,' he told her. ' I'll take it along to the kitchen, and you can have first bath.'

' Thanks,' she said huskily.

But in spite of her warm bath, and a change into one of the lovely plain dresses which Elizabeth had helped her to choose, she still felt rather young and insignificant beside Rosalie, who looked beautiful in palest lavender.

Elizabeth looked much better, and sparkled with laughter quite a lot, though Catherine felt that there was a brittle quality behind it all which was just as disturbing as her quiet listlessness.

She had invited another two men to make up numbers round the large dining table, and one of them, Simon Hamilton, was paying her lots of attention. The other one sat beside Catherine, and although he talked a great deal, his conversation seemed to go over her head. She couldn't even remember his name.

Instead she could only see the beautiful laughing face of Rosalie Craven, as she looked up at John whose dark head was bent towards her attentively. Again a wave of jealousy swept over her, and she felt sickened with herself. It was an emotion which was foreign to her, and which frightened and disgusted her. If John wanted Rosalie, then she should be happy for them both.

But over all the happy party, one face seemed to hover like a spectre. Michael Rodgers was not there, but Catherine could feel his presence, and knew that he was still in the minds of all four Sheridans. And especially Elizabeth.

On Wednesdays Catherine now went to evening classes to get practical experience for her F.G.A.

She now knew the properties of most gem stones, but she had to learn how to use a refractometer when testing for refractive index, and how to test in a practical way for specific gravity.

As she left the classes the following Wednesday and turned into the street, a figure stepped forward and called her name.

' Catherine! '

She jumped, startled.

' Michael! What are you doing here? '

' Waiting for you,' he told her quietly. ' You've been ages.'

' I had some tidying up to do.'

He had taken her arm and was walking along beside her.

' I want to talk to you, Kate. Can we go to that hotel where we had a meal together once upon a time? '

She hesitated.

' They'll wonder where I've got to.'

' Oh, for heaven's sake,' he cried impatiently, ' must you always be kow-towing to the Sheridans? Can't you even spare me an hour of your time? What's an hour out of a lifetime? '

She felt his need to talk to her, and her reluctance melted. She would telephone from the hotel in case Aunt Lucille was arranging a meal for her which would spoil.

' All right, Michael, I'll be glad to have a meal with you. I've been wondering what you were doing

. . . if you'd gone in with another firm or something.'

'Don't worry about me,' he laughed shortly. 'I'm all right, as they say. I knew it would come to this sooner or later, so I prepared for it. No, it's you I want to protect, Catherine. And I think there are a few things you ought to know about our friends the Sheridans.'

Her footsteps slowed.

'I . . . I don't think I want to listen to a lot of gossip and grumbles, Michael. I can make up my own mind about Uncle James and Aunt Lucille, . . . John and Elizabeth, too. They've all been wonderful to me. In fact, they've given me back my life. I know you have a private quarrel with them, but it's got nothing to do with me.'

His fingers bit into her arm.

'That's what you think. But I still want you to listen to what I have to say, *then* make up your mind, my dear. Believe me, I . . . I'm not doing it for fun.'

She walked beside him silently, then he asked, his voice ragged,

'How's Elizabeth?'

She considered before replying.

'*She* would say she's splendid, but I think she's very unhappy, Michael. She's so thin, and her appetite is poor. Aunt Lucille worries about her.'

'It's her own fault!' he said harshly. 'I couldn't even *begin* to talk to her!'

He escorted her into the hotel, and Catherine excused herself so that she could have a wash, and telephone. Aunt Lucille did not ask questions, and Catherine was glad of that as she put back the receiver and went to join Michael in the dining room.

' Please, not a lot this evening,' she pleaded. ' I —I don't feel very hungry.'

' Trying to be even thinner than Elizabeth?' he asked, and she would have been annoyed but for the fact that, now she had a good look at him, Michael looked rather gaunt and unhappy himself. If he had made a new life for himself, then it did not seem to be bringing him much pleasure.

He ordered omelettes for both of them, then leaned his elbows on the table, saying nothing.

' Have you got another partnership, then?' she asked at last.

' *Another* partnership? I was never a partner of any kind at Sheridan and Rodgers. James Sheridan bought my father out years ago, after he had worked like a slave to get that business on to its feet. He bought him out cheaply just before it all started to pay off. My father died soon afterwards, and James Sheridan offered to train me when I left school . . . as an employee, of course. My position has never been privileged.'

' I see,' said Catherine, watching his face.

' Do you? I wonder! He's demanded everything from my family. I saw my father . . . old, tired, in his grave years before his time, and I knew

144

I was going to get my own back on James Sheridan. So I founded my own company . . . Newclox . . . and I saw that it was on its feet before I left Sheridans. They used us, so I used them. . . .'

'So you really were to blame over . . . over some of the mistakes and the loss of sales!' cried Catherine.

'Do you blame me?'

She was silent, trying to take it all in.

'I had my mother to fight for. She never speaks about it, but she's better off now than she's ever been. She married again, of course. I'll take you to see her one day, Catherine.'

'Do you live with her?'

'No, I told you . . . she married again. Happily he's a good type, my stepfather. She's all right with him.'

'But Elizabeth,' she said, after they had again sat in silence. 'Why did you propose to Elizabeth, if you wanted nothing to do with them?'

This time it was Michael's turn to flush.

'I thought she was different. I thought that she could leave them, come with me . . . only I left it too late to explain to her, and when I tried she wouldn't listen. She thought I was a traitor, trying to ruin their business, while it appeared to be in my interest to build it up. I even tried to make her jealous sometimes by . . . well, never mind that. I only know that she hates me now.'

'I don't think she hates you,' said Catherine

quietly, 'but I don't think you could blame her either. It must look very different from her point of view.'

Michael gazed at her intently.

'And yours, Catherine?'

She drew a deep breath. Michael obviously believed that James Sheridan had used Frederick Rodgers . . . his health and energy . . . then discarded him before he could reap any benefits, and by doing so had also robbed his son of those benefits. He had kept Michael in the firm, but again he had used his natural skill and competence, and had only offered a normal salary as a reward.

Yet it was difficult to see Uncle James in this role. He was kindly and thoughtful, and he had given her a home and a job. He would probably have given Michael a partnership of some kind when he married Elizabeth, and he had also had no objection, obviously, to accepting Michael into his family.

Catherine was shaking her head. She couldn't accept Uncle James as a villain. Nor had John ever uttered a word of criticism regarding Michael, except to see that Elizabeth's interests were protected.

'I think there's misunderstanding somewhere,' she said slowly. 'I don't think Uncle James realises you feel this way, Michael. Perhaps he could give you his point of view. . . .'

'And very plausible it would be,' said Michael bitterly. 'I knew you would say that. You're sitting there all ripe for plucking yourself, and I've done you a favour by telling you. There was a time when I even thought I would *like* to take you out of it all. Especially when Elizabeth was going all superior on me. I could feel your attraction, and I thought I could make you interested. . . .' He paused and looked at her. ' Was I wrong?' he asked softly, and she shook her head.

' No, I was attracted,' she said honestly, ' but it was a fleeting thing which didn't last. Instead I . . .'

' I know,' he said harshly. ' You fell for John. Good old John, who's got it made for practically everything in his life. All he wants he can have. It would do him good to rough it for a while.'

' Don't be so bitter,' she said sharply. ' John's path isn't as smooth as you imagine. He does work for what he has, and he always will.'

' I won't argue with you,' he told her, sighing a little. ' Anyway, I know how you feel. It . . . it takes a while to get them out of the blood.'

He ordered coffee in the lounge and escorted Catherine to a quiet corner where it was warm and comfortable, though she hardly saw her surroundings. None of this seemed to be real.

She thought of Elizabeth and knew that she still loved Michael. Yet what hope would there be for either of them if, all the time, he had been hating her family for years? There must have been times when he had softened towards them, when he had fallen in love with Elizabeth. Because he *did* love her, and *still* did, thought Catherine, looking at him. How ironic for him that this should have happened.

But now he had his own business . . . Newclox. Elizabeth had wondered about that place, probably feeling instinctively that there was something odd about it. Catherine was even now remembering Michael's absences from the shop, when he claimed to be delivering and setting up wall clocks. No doubt he was also spending some time making sure his own business was proceeding satisfactorily.

Sudden distaste for the whole affair took hold of her, and she drank her coffee quickly.

' I must get back, Michael,' she told him, quickly. ' I . . . I'm sorry everything has been so . . . sort of . . . upset for you. No doubt Uncle James will find out about your own business and will be hurt . . . if you wanted to hurt him. No doubt Elizabeth . . .'

' Elizabeth knows! '

' *Oh!* '

So *that* was why she was taking it so hard. She thought that Michael had betrayed them all, not only her.

' I must go then,' she said coldly. ' I . . . there's no need to wish you every success. I'm sure you'll see that you get it.'

' Sit down! ' he said, rather curtly.

' No, I'm sorry. I'll go now. . . .'

' Sit down. Please, Catherine. Can you tell me

what happened to your pearl?'

She stared at him, then sat down.

'My what?'

'Your pearl . . . the one your father found.'
This time it was his turn to stare. 'You don't know
about it? They haven't told you, or asked you
yet? I thought he was just biding his time, then the
publicity campaign would start, and he would be
exhibiting a pearl even bigger than the Abernethy.
Not that it would have done him much good without
all the other pearl jewellery to back it up, but I knew
he would think of something. I mean, a pearl like
that . . . its value would be fabulous.'

'I don't understand a word you say,' she said
flatly. 'What on earth are you talking about?'

'That does surprise me. I don't know how dear
James could contain himself while you went through
all your personal papers. It must be still among
your stuff somewhere. He made sure that your
father hadn't got rid of it, especially when he was
so keen to buy it himself. He made your father an
offer.'

'Start at the beginning, please,' said Catherine,
her heart thumping. 'I'm completely in the dark.'

'Didn't you know your father had found a fabulous pearl and took it with him when he went to
London? Only he made the mistake of calling on
his old friend James Sheridan, in Newcastle, and
of showing it to John and me as well. It was a
whopper. James was panting to buy it, but your

149

father rather put him off. He had other plans, I think. Probably he felt obliged to offer his normal firm first refusal.

' But a few days later he was dead, and James went to see your mother. It was obvious she knew nothing about it, or if she did, she was keeping quiet. So he very cleverly offered to give her advice about any business she found difficult to deal with, and in particular his finding of pearls. James said he would see to all that for her.

' However, time went on, and he was foxed. Did she know about it? Or did she know nothing? I don't know how he managed to keep silent . . . some crafty purpose of his own . . . but when the accident happened and . . . and only you were left, he offered to sort out your affairs.'

She nodded, fascinated.

' He brought down all personal papers, and no doubt he's been trying to contain himself in patience, waiting for you to run to him one day, with the pearl in your hands, wondering if it's at all valuable. Oh, he'll give you *something* for it, but it will bring him far more than he gives you. He might even keep it in the family by marrying you off to John.'

Her face went white.

' That's enough!' she cried. ' You go too far.'

' You can't tell me John hasn't been interested in you. It's only a matter of time till he proposes. The Cravens were all right, but dear Rosalie will want more *out* of the Sheridans than she'll bring with her. Poor old John designed her a pretty little ring, and you should have seen her face! She'd thought she would have her pick of the diamonds! I felt sorry for him then, because that was when he saw through her.'

Catherine wasn't smiling.

' I know nothing about a pearl,' she said quietly, ' and if there had been one, I'm afraid I *would* have known about it by now. Father would have told us.'

' Did he have time? I thought he was taken ill as soon as he got home. I remember thinking the excitement had gone for him, poor chap.'

She was silent. There *had* been no time. She remembered the fear and anguish of getting him to bed, and the doctor, and how quickly he seemed to go.

After that she and her mother had managed as best they could. Alison had never discussed business with her, but sometimes she had said it would be all right, and she would have a lovely surprise on her wedding day . . .

Remembering, Catherine could only manage a twisted smile. How dreadful that sounded now! But could Alison have been going to give her the pearl as a wedding gift? It would be just like her to make that sort of gesture.

Only, if so, where was it? She had been through everything, and Uncle James had questioned her casually about that. If there *had* been a pearl, wouldn't he have encouraged her to search more thoroughly? Wouldn't he have *told* her?

She put her head in her hands.

' I must go, Michael. All this . . . I must think about it. You've . . . it doesn't seem real. I don't know what to believe now.'

His face softened.

' Sorry, my dear, but I had to tell you. They aren't going to exploit you, too, as they did me. You watch out for yourself, now that you know about it. And if you find that pearl, and want advice, then you can come to me.'

' Thank you,' she said shakily, ' but my father had an excellent outlet for his pearls. I can't imagine him taking it anywhere else for valuation. There must be some other explanation.'

' Well, maybe so. But either he has it somewhere, or the money for it. Either way, you're quite well off, Catherine. Just remember that.'

She listened, but she couldn't believe. Almost in a dream she walked out of the hotel, and Michael drove her home, not caring if the Sheridans saw him or not.

' I shan't come in,' he said, with a rather twisted smile.

' Goodnight,' she said mechanically, and hurried up the drive, letting herself in with her own key.

John met her in the hall.

' Catherine! I've been wondering. . . .'

' I've got a headache, John,' she interrupted,

rather wildly. 'I'll go straight up to bed. Say goodnight to everyone for me, will you?'

She ran on upstairs, aware of his eyes following her till she closed the bedroom door, then she prepared mechanically for bed, and lay between the sheets, her eyes hot and sandy when she tried to close them.

It was hours before she fell asleep.

CHAPTER IX

Catherine woke unrefreshed next morning, and decided that she would speak to Uncle James without delay, and clear up the suspicions which Michael had put into her mind. She came down to breakfast feeling composed and purposeful, but everyone was in rather a hurry, and Elizabeth only appeared at the last moment.

Catherine paused as she looked at the other girl, her eyes suddenly full of concern. Elizabeth looked very pale as she quickly drank a cup of black coffee, then picked up her bag.

'Elizabeth!' she called.

'Yes?'

'Are you sure you're quite well?'

'Quite well,' said Elizabeth crisply, then as she turned to go out of the door, Catherine saw her fumble with the doorknob, then she ran to hold the other girl as her body slumped against the door. Uncle James was there almost before her, shouting to John, and it was John who carried his sister back upstairs to bed.

It was a disrupted, difficult morning. After making sure that Aunt Lucille and Mrs Bannon could cope, and ringing for the doctor, they had to leave for business, knowing that Miss Pryce and Mrs Neal would be waiting for the keys.

Uncle James rang home shortly after they were organised, and Catherine wasn't surprised to hear that Elizabeth had nervous exhaustion, and would have to be quiet for several days. She had not been eating well, and the lack of food had weakened her physically.

'Can you cope, do you think?' Uncle James asked Catherine anxiously. 'I'll get someone new straight away . . . a young man, I think, who could train for Michael's job, when . . . when Elizabeth is better.'

'I'm sure Miss Pryce and I can cope,' Catherine assured him, feeling sorry for James Sheridan. All of a sudden he seemed older, and she saw John viewing him with concern.

'We're well organised, Dad,' John told him, 'and Catherine is no passenger nowadays. She learns fast.'

He gave her his warm smile, and she found herself responding, then she turned away and went to talk to Miss Pryce. If everything Michael had told her was the truth, then she would have to put John Sheridan out of her mind and heart.

In fact, she wouldn't be staying here, she thought rather wretchedly, looking round the lovely showroom which had become so familiar to her, and which she had begun to love. She now knew practically every piece of jewellery in the place, and she was sometimes consulted over stock when a representative called from the dealers in fine diamonds in Hatton Garden.

Catherine now had quite a shrewd idea as to the demand for pearl and diamond earrings and brooches, and could select the ones most suited to her customers. She enjoyed this, and often felt a flow of pleasure when her own choice was sold soon after selection.

Now she and Miss Pryce quickly organised their day so that they could work together without treading on one another's toes. Miss Pryce was most concerned about Elizabeth, and Catherine realised how fond the older woman was of the girl.

'She takes things too hard,' she said, her bright dark eyes anxious. 'That's always been Elizabeth's trouble. She tries to pretend she doesn't care. I used to think she was jealous of you . . .'

'There was no need. There *is* no need,' Catherine amended.

'I know that now, but for a time I wondered.'

Catherine said nothing more, and Miss Pryce took the hint and dropped the subject.

Nevertheless the days were busy, even though a new young man was employed to start on Monday. He would be working under John, and he seemed a cheerful boy when he called to have his interview.

'I expect I'll be tea boy,' he confided to Catherine, as he waited for James Sheridan to see him in the office. 'I'm an expert at that.'

'I hope you'll also be an expert at behaving yourself,' Miss Pryce told him sternly. 'We've had expert tea boys before who forgot to wash their hands properly, and left sticky fingermarks on the best watches.'

Ian Adams held out clean hands.

' I don't bite my fingernails either,' he said, as he rose suddenly, being quickly summoned into the office.

' I don't know what lads are coming to these days,' said Miss Pryce, though her eyes were twinkling. ' The last one imitated a customer in a funny hat by putting the wash leather on his head, just out of range at the back of the shop. Only she saw him reflected in the mirror!'

' Oh dear,' said Catherine.

' Yes . . . Oh, dear!'

On Saturday Elizabeth was looking a little stronger, and John came to find Catherine. He had been speaking on the telephone, no doubt to Rosalie.

' I think we have a date,' he informed her. ' We could go out for a meal, then on to a symphony concert. It's mainly Beethoven, and I can just about manage that.'

' You mean we're going with someone . . . with a party?'

' No, just you and me,' he said firmly, ' on our own.'

' Oh . . . well . . .'

' I'm flattered that you leap at the chance of going with me,' he told her ruefully, and she couldn't help smiling.

'Oh, all right, John. I'll be ready in a moment. I'll just see if Elizabeth is O.K.'

'She can have Rosalie Craven to talk to. She's coming round in a short while. Hurry up, Kate, do.'

Catherine hurried, her mind busy. John was running away again, and at one time she had felt annoyed that he just did not stand up and put Rosalie in her place.

But there was no doubt that the other girl was very difficult to shake off, as she had been when she got to know her better. John wasn't soft, and sooner or later he could turn into a mass of iron when driven too far.

But he hated hurting people. Catherine had seen that, too, when he had been thoughtless in the house, and had suddenly been made to realise it.

Now Catherine's mind was turning again to Michael Rodgers. It had been on her mind such a lot, and she had not been able to talk it over with anyone. Perhaps she could find an opportunity to talk it over with John.

It was obvious to John that Catherine's mind was not wholly on the concert. She had talked and laughed during the evening, but always her eyes had become grave and questioning as they looked at him, and he felt it was time to speak about their future once again. Perhaps, by now, Catherine would have had time to think about his proposal, and

158

nerves gripped him when he thought that her answer might now be very different.

As he led her back to the car, the warmth of the evening and the beauty of the music he had just heard still with him, John was very silent, but he quickly drove to a quiet place he knew quite near home, and stopped the car, then turned to Catherine.

'I . . . I've got to ask you, Catherine . . .' he began.

'And I've got to ask you,' she interrupted, 'something very important.'

'What?' he asked, his heart racing.

'Is it true that my father found a rather wonderful pearl just before he died?'

John felt his heart sink with disappointment, and Catherine could almost feel the life go out of him. So it *was* true!

'Yes,' he told her quietly. 'Have you found it, dear? I . . . I'm very glad for you. We were afraid . . .'

'So *that* was it!' she cried. Somehow it had not seemed quite real until now, but if Michael had been right about that, then he was probably right about everything else.

'That was it,' she repeated. 'You all wanted me because you knew I've got something of value. And I was stupid enough to think you . . . you wanted me for myself.'

'But, Catherine, I *do* . . .'

'Don't try to make it better by lying to me, John,'

she said. 'Is it also true that your father bought out Mr Rodgers just when the firm was getting on its feet?'

'Who told you that? Who's been speaking to you?'

'Who else could have told me but Michael himself. I . . . I didn't believe what he told me, but now I do. Now I believe that you use people for your own ends, you and Uncle James. What will you do now that I've gone over all Dad's things, and I can't find the pearl? Throw me out, as you've thrown Michael out?'

'No,' said John icily. 'I'm going to take you home. Obviously I can't talk to you while you throw all these wild accusations at me . . . and my father. You've listened to Mike Rodgers, and accepted all he said for gospel. Yet one thing we do ask of our employees is loyalty, and we've been having precious little from him.'

'Only because you forced it on him. He had learned to protect his interests.'

'Is that what you believe? Is that why my sister has worried herself sick . . . really sick! She's pretty straight-dealing herself, and it was his treachery which threw Elizabeth. *That's* what she can't get over. I don't think even Father realises that, though I do. I know her pretty well, and it's no good asking me to have sympathy for Mike Rodgers.'

John had gone cold and hard again in his anger,

and Catherine sat beside him, miserably, as he started up the car engine again. His anger was mixed with keen disappointment that his hopes had disappeared in a hurl of accusations.

' I'll see Uncle James tomorrow,' said Catherine. ' I expect he'll want me to go. I don't know what Dad can have done with the pearl, so if you and he wanted it for your own ends, I'm sorry to disappoint you.'

' You may not have the pearl, but you've certainly got imagination. I suppose it's no use telling you that we thought we were protecting your interests, that we took you to live with us because we wanted you, and that I consider it fine reward if you walk out now, just when you're beginning to be responsible enough to be of use to the firm. We no longer have Michael, which is no doubt an asset rather than anything else, though he did work sometimes.

' Elizabeth is ill, and my father beginning to feel his age, as I've no doubt Prycey is too, though she would murder me for saying so. The boy is so new that he hardly knows one gem stone from another. So if you want to walk out, do so. No doubt Mike's got a nice job all lined up for you, and can afford to offer you a higher salary than we can.'

He had stopped the car, and the front door of the house was dancing up and down before the tears in her eyes.

Quickly she blinked them away as she got out of the car, then inside the house they were forgotten as

Lucille met them in the hall.

'Oh, I'm glad you're back,' she greeted them. 'I . . . I'm afraid Elizabeth is rather ill again. She . . . she said she felt so much better and wanted to come downstairs, so . . . so I let her. Only I was so busy getting everything ready for her, I forgot to tell her not to come down on her own and . . . and she fell down the stairs. She must have had a giddy spell again. James is with her now, and there's a nurse coming. I . . . I thought you were the nurse.'

John's eyes met Catherine's, and together they went to Lucille.

'It's all right, darling, we'll take care of everything. Obviously she's not so bad, or the doctor would have moved her to hospital.'

'There's nothing broken, but she's bruised and shocked.'

'Can I see her?' asked Catherine.

'I expect so. Just for a moment. Oh, John, there's the nurse now.'

Catherine ran on upstairs before the nurse took charge, feeling that she wanted to see Elizabeth, if only for a moment. There was a great pain in her heart, which she had thought was anger at how she herself had been treated, but now it was for Elizabeth . . . and not a little for John. She had seen the anguish in his eyes as they looked at her, and she knew that in spite of everything, she loved him. And she loved Elizabeth, too. She loved her courage and self-discipline, and she felt compassion for her now that the courage which had made her get out of bed and try to face everything again had led her to further pain and illness.

Uncle James looked up tiredly when she slipped silently into the bedroom. Elizabeth had a bruise on her cheek, and her eyes were closed.

' She's still sleeping,' he said. ' The doctor gave her something.'

' The nurse is here,' said Catherine softly.

' Well, thank goodness for that. She'll take proper care of her. The doctor says she's been very lucky. I . . . we think she only fell a few steps, and the stairs are broad and shallow. It could have been a lot worse.'

' Was it a giddy spell?'

' Either that or she tripped on that long robe of hers. We don't know. Lucille only heard her fall, and Mrs Bannon was upstairs in the bathroom. Elizabeth should have waited, and not come down by herself.'

A moment later Lucille appeared with the nurse, a cheerful robust woman who quickly took charge. Catherine took another long look at Elizabeth before she left the room, and knew that this certainly was not the time to have things out with Uncle James. That would have to wait till Elizabeth was a great deal better.

The days were busy ones, and in the evenings Catherine spent some time sitting beside Elizabeth's bed and telling her about any amusing incidents which had happened during the day.

Quite a few of the representatives who called regularly were now friends, and they would send their best wishes to her for a speedy recovery. Catherine always tried to make her visits as bright as possible and soon she felt that Elizabeth looked forward to her coming. She was careful never to mention Michael's name, or to discuss the pearl her father had found, in case it brought him into the conversation.

'I still ache all over,' Elizabeth told her ruefully one evening. 'I feel such a fool that I should fall downstairs like that.'

'What happened?' Catherine asked.

'That's the funny part—I just don't remember. I remember thinking I'd had enough of bed, and deciding to come downstairs for an hour or two, then . . . well, I must have knocked myself out.'

'Well, don't worry about it or Nurse will put me out.'

They looked at each other and grinned, just as John put his head round the door. His face changed when he saw Catherine, and she stood up, her smile sobering.

'I'll go now, Elizabeth. John can take my place.'

'I've no wish to chase you away.'

'I was going anyway,' she said crisply. 'I have things I must attend to.'

She heard Elizabeth's clear voice asking what was

wrong as she closed the door, and she felt chagrined. John had caught her off guard. They had no wish to bother Elizabeth with their private quarrel, she was sure. No doubt John would soon set her mind at rest, however.

In her own room Catherine began, again, to look through her personal possessions, this time with a much clearer eye, now that she knew why she was searching. Uncle James had impressed on her, previously, that she must not throw anything away, unless she was sure it wasn't needed, and she now knew why this was so. Remembering, she had no fears that she had inadvertently thrown the pearl away.

It hadn't been among her father's personal things. She had helped her mother to go through everything, and her mother had sent everything to a charity.

Now all the papers were tidy, and much easier to examine, as were other personal things such as old pieces of jewellery and watches in a jewellery box, some favourite ornaments now on the mantelpiece, books, her father's old pipes and tobacco jar, also on the mantelpiece.

Catherine peered into the tobacco jar, and wondered if she ought to throw out the small amount of tobacco which was left. Her mother had just kept such personal things as they were, probably taking comfort from having them there.

Catherine got a newspaper and tipped out the tobacco, since it was the one place she had not yet looked. It hadn't seemed necessary before she knew about the pearl, but now everywhere must be searched.

Her heart bounded when she saw the tissue paper, and her fingers trembled as she opened it up and looked at the pearl. It was very beautiful, but a second careful scrutiny showed her that it wasn't quite so perfect as the one she had seen in Perth. Nevertheless, it was probably very valuable, and she wrapped it up carefully again, and put it back where she had found it. She must think about all this, wondering if her mother had once done that very thing, or if she had never known about it at all. At the moment her mind seemed to be scarcely working at all.

Why hadn't Uncle James told her? Why hadn't he asked about the pearl? She could easily have thrown out the jar, and lost it for ever.

But no . . . he knew she would never part with any of her father's things. She remembered that she wanted to keep everything when he offered to attend to the removal and storage of her furniture. Perhaps he wanted to look for it himself! Was that it? And when he didn't find it, he encouraged her to look through everything carefully, knowing that sooner or later she would find it. He would know that her father hadn't sold the pearl, or the find would have become widely known.

She puzzled over it for a long time, until Aunt Lucille came to ask her if she was feeling all right, and if she wouldn't like a hot drink before bedtime.

'Coming,' said Catherine. 'I . . . I'm sorry, Aunt Lucille. I've been rather busy, tidying up.'

'Try to get to bed early, then,' said Aunt Lucille comfortably. 'John has gone out, too. Another late night for him, probably. I don't know what's come over everyone these days.'

Uncle James was downstairs, and he looked up with his usual smile when Catherine came in.

'Hello, my dear. Come and sit here by the fireside.'

'I'm quite warm, thank you, Uncle James.'

'Oh.' He looked at her whimsically. 'I was rather thinking that you seemed a bit cool these days, Catherine. It would be nice to think I'm wrong.'

She bit her lip, then coloured at the implication of his words. Then she looked him straight in the eye.

'I've found the pearl, Uncle James. It was in the tobacco jar.'

His face registered surprise and delight.

'Well, congratulations, my dear. I *thought* you would find it sooner or later. Did John decide to tell you about it after all?'

'No,' she said evenly. 'Michael Rodgers told me.'

'Michael!' James Sheridan stared at her, then his eyes became concerned. 'What did he tell you, Catherine?'

'Everything.'

Her hands were shaking a little, because suddenly she was getting reaction, and having to keep a tight hold on herself.

' He told me about how you had bought out his father, just when the business started to pay, and now he's got the sack. And he told me about . . . about the pearl and . . . everything. . . .'

She couldn't think straight, aware of his eyes on her, then she looked at him squarely, and was disconcerted to see only the usual kindness and compassion on his face. There was no anger, as there had been with John.

' Michael has only been telling you half truths, Catherine,' he told her. ' It's a long story, my dear, but I would like to tell you what really happened. I had hoped only Michael's mother and himself, also John and I would be the only people to hear about poor old Freddy Rodgers, but when Michael goes distorting things to suit himself, then I must put it right.'

He pulled up a chair for her, and she sat down obediently, near the fire. She would listen to what Uncle James had to say, but would it be the truth? Obviously it was to be a different story from Michael's, and she had felt that Michael believed, firmly, every word he had told her. He had sworn it was true.

Yet it was hard to believe that James Sheridan wasn't also telling the truth. . . .

'Freddie and I started this business together when we came out of the Army. We were both married, with a son . . . Elizabeth was born a year later . . . and we had such plans for our families. It was hard work, but we put our heads down and got on with it. I had already trained in the buying and selling of diamonds, and Freddie was a watchmaker who was skilled at mending watches and clocks.

'We took chances, but gradually Freddie wanted to take more chances than I did. He was a gambler, though at the time I didn't realise how much of a gambler he was. He used to listen to racing results on a small radio he kept at the back of the shop, and I often teased him about losing his shilling.'

James Sheridan sighed, his eyes rather bleak.

'Only it wasn't a shilling, Catherine. It . . . was a great deal more. I knew little about it at first, until Joan Rodgers came to see Lucille one day. She was in distress, and we learned the true state of Freddie's home life. He was deeply in debt, all things of value having been sold, and Joan was in despair, wondering which way to turn for necessities.

'Fortunately the financial side of our business was conducted in such a way that Freddie couldn't draw out more than his share of the profits, or I dare say it would have been lost for both of us. The four of us . . . he and Joan, Lucille and myself . . . sat down and worked things out till we had a true picture of his finances, and I think we were all very shocked. Especially Freddy. He was a cheerful, lovable man, but for him gambling had become a disease. His little " flutters " had grown and grown till it grew into something he couldn't handle. One could not blame him, Catherine. It's a . . . a form of illness in much the same way as alcoholism. It's one of the worst for the family to bear.

' Freddy offered a solution, and asked me to buy him out. He wanted to wipe the slate clean, and try to start afresh, and it was quite a setback to Lucille and me, trying to find the money to give to Freddie. Lucille had a little money of her own, which she insisted on putting into the kitty, and I parted with some things I had hoped never to lose . . . old books and pictures which I have never been able to replace. The rest we borrowed.'

Catherine said nothing. She watched James Sheridan and knew that she was hearing exactly what had happened all those years ago.

' It's true that the business was just beginning to pay. Perhaps in some ways that was unfair to Freddie, but we didn't see it like that at the time. We had no real means of knowing that success lay ahead.

' At any rate, Lucille and I made a great effort and gradually we came out on top. Freddie set aside a room in his house and kept on mending clocks and watches, and letting Joan manage things for him. We sent him as much work as we could and sometimes, we knew, the old disease would break out and he would keep having to make fresh starts.

'I went to see him as often as I could, hoping to help. But he changed, and became bitter. Then he was ill and . . . well, he died.'

James sighed.

'The children were growing up. We helped Joan as best we could, and after a time she married again. Michael grew into a fine boy, and when I used to remember the plans Freddie and I made for our sons, I offered him a position in the firm.

'Even in those days, I . . . I felt he and Elizabeth would . . .' James broke off again, his face hardening suddenly. 'I didn't know he had his own plans made . . . behind my back!' he said harshly. 'He was using his position in the firm for his own ends. I can't imagine his mother would know. Joan's a fine woman, and was always grateful for any help we tried to give. She's moved from the old house now. We've rather lost touch with her, but we used to send her our fondest regards . . . through Michael. I wonder if she ever got them!'

There was a long silence while Catherine sat quietly by the fireside. She thought of Michael's dark unhappy eyes and how convinced he was that the Sheridans had cheated his family. Did he have a point in that James Sheridan had reaped the benefit of years of work done by his father? Yet his father could so easily have ruined the business entirely.

'Does Michael know? That his father had gambled away his share of the business?'

171

Uncle James frowned.

'Of course. At least, he knew his father had to sell out for financial reasons. I don't know how much his mother told him when he was old enough to understand. . . .'

His frown deepened as he stared at Catherine.

'We made no secret of it to him. Though, of course, any time I spoke to Michael about his father, it was mainly about the happy times in our association. But he knew why the partnership had been dissolved.'

'But he believes you took his best years of hard work, then bought him out just *before* the business became prosperous. He believes that was a form of cheating.'

'His mother wouldn't allow him to believe that.'

'I should have thought his mother would say nothing to cast reflection on his father's memory.'

James was leaning forward.

'No,' he said slowly, 'that's true. I . . . I suppose I never really thought about it. Time has gone past, and for me the early struggles of those days have dimmed down. And they were struggles, believe me. And it never occurred to me that it could be different for Michael . . . that he had, in fact, been nursing this grudge. I . . . I thought he would become like another son to me, when he married Elizabeth. I thought he really loved her, even as children.'

Uncle James sat tapping the arm of his chair, and

Catherine leaned forward.

' Couldn't you tell him the truth?' she asked gently, and watched a slow flush mount his cheeks.

' He shouldn't have to be told anything,' he said angrily. ' He's been treated honourably and decently ever since he came into the firm. I was willing to trust him with my daughter's happiness. If that wasn't enough for him, I don't know what was. Why should I go crawling to him to make him think well of me? He would only accuse me of trying to blacken his father!'

Catherine nodded. This was probably true. It looked as though there was a great misunderstanding between Michael Rodgers and the Sheridans, and it was insurmountable.

Only Elizabeth was in the middle.

' Not even for Elizabeth's sake?' she asked gently.

' Especially for her sake. I can no longer trust that young man. Elizabeth will get over him. She's young enough.'

But Elizabeth felt things so deeply, thought Catherine, and her thoughts turned to John. Perhaps she could appeal to him to help. Somehow it seemed cruel that two young people could be so unhappy because of things that had happened in the past. Because she was now convinced that Michael's heart was aching as much as Elizabeth's.

She rose. ' I think I'll go to bed, Uncle James.'

' All right, my dear. Oh, if you care to let me see your pearl again. . . .'

The pearl! Her face paled a little, and she sat down again suddenly.

'Why didn't you tell me about it? Did Mother know?'

Again he looked at her levelly.

'I don't know, but looking back, I don't think so. Though I couldn't be sure of that at the time. You see, your father said he had plans for that pearl, but didn't say what they were. Remembering my experience with Freddie. . . .'

James Sheridan's cheeks suddenly coloured again, and Catherine could sense his embarrassment.

'You see, my dear, I thought I knew Freddie so well, but I didn't know him at all. I had no idea he was such a gambler. So that when your father wouldn't discuss the pearl, I . . . I didn't want to pry too deeply. Later . . . well, I wondered if it hadn't gone to meet some liabilities, which I knew nothing about, and I didn't want to ask your mother in case it upset her in any way.

'David said it was a secret from her, as yet. That's the last we heard. Suppose I had asked her, and her hopes had been raised, then she had found that the pearl had been used for . . . well, something. Wouldn't that have been upsetting?

'So I decided it wasn't my affair. I offered to help her in any way I could, as I had done with Joan. I encouraged her to take a holiday, knowing you were all right with the Neills.

'Then . . . later . . . when that tragic business

happened, I encouraged you to come here, and to go through things carefully . . . just in case. I was sure Alison would come to me if she found it, or would tell me if she had sold it elsewhere. You see?'

'I see,' said Catherine slowly, then she looked at him levelly. 'Will you want to buy the pearl, Uncle James?'

His eyes twinkled.

'Only if you really want to sell it, and I think your father's old market for his pearl should have first refusal, don't you? I can hardly start a new line with one pearl.'

Her eyes cleared and she bent forward and kissed his cheek.

'Uncle James, I don't deserve you. I'm sorry.'

'For what?'

'Lots and lots, but it's getting late. I must go up now.'

'All right, my dear. Goodnight.'

As she mounted the stairs, the front door opened, and John came into the hall. For a long moment they stared at one another, but Catherine saw no softening of his mouth.

Perhaps he had been out with Rosalie, she thought. Perhaps it cheered him to know that one girl wanted him. Miss Pryce had hinted that she also wanted the diamonds he could give her, but perhaps it wasn't true, and Rosalie now knew she really loved John.

' Goodnight,' she called huskily.

She wanted to apologise to him for doubting their motives in taking her into their home.

' Goodnight,' he said crisply, and she went on up to bed.

CHAPTER X

Elizabeth's improvement was very slow, and some days she looked pale and depressed. Catherine saw that Aunt Lucille was worried about her, but the older woman maintained a cheerful attitude towards her, and had long talks with the doctor in private. As soon as Elizabeth was able to get up, Lucille planned to take her abroad for a month or two.

'Not too far away, Mother,' pleaded Elizabeth, who had agreed to her plans, as much to make her mother happy as to improve her own health. 'I don't feel like travelling too far afield . . .'

'Not the Channel Islands again, dear,' protested Lucille, who loved going there, but who felt that somewhere different was called for. Elizabeth must be taken out of herself.

Catherine enjoyed sitting in on the discussions, but she herself was feeling restless and dissatisfied with her life at the moment. Nothing seemed to be going right. John was considerate and polite towards her, but she felt that a coolness had grown between them, a sort of barrier which just wouldn't go away, even though she had told him, haltingly, that she had been mistaken.

'I'm glad you feel that,' he told her gravely. 'I'm glad you don't feel that my father and I conceal horns under our hair.'

But their friendship had undergone a change, and now John treated her warily, and she longed for the old teasing affection. Yet perhaps that affection might be just as bad as indifference. It would be a far cry from love.

If only she could clear things up between Elizabeth and Michael, she thought unhappily. That, at least, might be something accomplished. Yet if she saw Michael again, he would only think she was being hoodwinked by the Sheridans. And she could only make him try to see the truth by telling him what James Sheridan had told her about his father. She couldn't possibly do that, thought Catherine, her whole being shrinking from such a thing. The only person who could, perhaps, tell him would be his mother.

His mother. He had promised to take Catherine to meet his mother one day, pointing out the pretty bungalow where she lived with his stepfather, as he drove Catherine home in his car one day. Michael now lived in a small flat, above the shop which she now knew was his.

On Wednesday evenings as she returned from evening classes on the bus, Catherine looked at the bungalow. Would it do any harm for her to see Mrs Rodgers, who was now Mrs Someone Else? Catherine did not even know her new name.

She dismissed the idea almost as soon as it was born. No doubt Michael's mother would be very angry at her interference. Yet as the days slipped

by, and she saw Elizabeth getting slowly better, but
still unhappy, her old courage and pride no longer
being worn like a proud flag, Catherine felt her
resolution being strengthened. What had she to
lose? If Michael's mother asked her to go, then she
could bear the humiliation, and Elizabeth would be
no worse off.

The following evening she gathered her courage together and caught the bus out to the bungalow, her
knees shaking a little as she walked through the
white-painted gate and up the flagged path.
Michael's stepfather must be a keen gardener, she
decided, looking at the neat borders and plentiful
flowers.

The woman who came to the door was so like
Michael that for a moment Catherine could only
stare, then she recovered enough to introduce herself.

'I'm Catherine Lyall, and I live with the Sheridans. I . . . I worked with Michael before he . . .
before he left the firm.'

'Of course. Michael has talked of you many
times. Please come in, Miss Lyall. Michael rather
forgot to tell me he was bringing you, and he said
he would be here after eight-thirty, so do forgive me
if I'm not quite ready to receive visitors yet.'

She was picking up discarded newspapers and a
pair of comfortable slippers, but Catherine scarcely
noticed.

' Michael . . . coming later?' she asked. ' Oh

dear, I didn't know. I'm afraid he won't want to find me here, Mrs . . .'

'Duncan. Joan Duncan.'

'Mrs Duncan. In fact, I don't think you would welcome me either, if you knew why I had come. Perhaps it would be better if I just go. . . .'

Mrs Duncan looked puzzled and a little alarmed.

'That sounds rather ominous, Miss Lyall. I think I would prefer to hear why you have come. Do sit down.'

Catherine sat down slowly, and rather gingerly, on the edge of a deep armchair, then drew a deep breath.

'Because of Elizabeth,' she said simply. 'She and Michael. There's such misunderstanding between them. I don't know how it could ever be unravelled. Yet Elizabeth is so unhappy, and I bet Michael is, too. So I thought that . . . well, you could help, Mrs Duncan. You know the whole story. At least, Uncle James said you did. Only Michael seems to have got it wrong.'

'Got what wrong?'

Catherine bit her lip, very embarrassed.

'About his father,' she said quietly, and the older woman stiffened.

'He thinks James Sheridan cheated his father after years of hard work, when he bought him out. Only Uncle James says it wasn't quite like that. There were . . . other reasons that you'd know about.'

She shot a glance at Mrs Duncan's stony face, and rushed almost blindly into the whole story, about what Michael had told her, how she had tackled James Sheridan and even about her own pearl.

'I had to ask Uncle James,' she said at length, 'and I feel he was telling me the truth. Only it's keeping them apart . . . Elizabeth and Michael . . . . if they each see a different side of the coin. If . . . if Michael doesn't know the *real* truth, couldn't he be told, Mrs Duncan?'

The older woman got up and walked nervously over to the window.

'And of course you believe what James Sheridan told you,' she said flatly.

Catherine paused only for a moment.

'Yes.'

Mrs Duncan hugged her arms, looking out at the pretty garden, then she sighed.

'And you'd be right,' she said at length. 'My first reaction to your coming here, Miss Lyall, *was* to ask you to leave, but you're good at putting your case. I know Michael has broken with Elizabeth and I've been trying to pretend it didn't matter. I've kept out of his life . . . perhaps afraid of the truth coming out, as it has . . . and out of his affair with Elizabeth for that very reason. But—well, I admire her very much.

'I knew, sooner or later, that Michael would break free, however. I thought I had no business to interfere, especially when the idolised image he has of his father comes from me.'

She came and sat down opposite Catherine.

' Does one tell a boy that his father was a gambler, and brought suffering to his wife and son because of it? If Freddy had lived, Mike would have found out for himself. But he didn't, and Mike only remembered him with love, and respect. I couldn't spoil that.'

' But when he quarrelled with Elizabeth . . .'

' He didn't say why they had quarrelled. I . . . rather wondered if he found you attractive.'

Catherine coloured.

' No, there was nothing like that between us, though . . . well, I thought he was very attractive when I first met him.'

Mrs Duncan smiled.

' Yes. There have been other girls making excuses to call, but for him it was always Elizabeth. That's why I was surprised. But, as I say, sometimes people change as they grow older. I wondered if Michael had changed. He was, all of a sudden, so . . . busy, somehow!'

' No doubt due to coming out in the open about his own business,' said Catherine dryly, and Mrs Duncan flushed.

' Yes, I should have told him, when I knew what he had done. Only I felt it was too late then.'

Catherine glanced at her watch. She would have to go before Michael arrived.

' I'd better go, then,' she said, standing up. ' You

know the position then, Mrs Duncan. I . . . I suppose it's up to you whether you decide to help or not. But I feel only you can do it.'

'I'll think about it,' Mrs Duncan told her.

'Is Michael's future happiness less important than his image of the past?' she asked quietly.

'I'll have to assure myself that it *is* his future happiness which is at stake,' Mrs Duncan returned smoothly, and opened the front door.

Catherine turned to shake hands, then her heart leapt into her mouth as the gate clicked and a tall figure swung up the steps.

'Catherine! What on earth are you doing here?' asked Michael.

She went scarlet.

'Er . . . you pointed out the bungalow to me once, Michael. I . . . I was rather at a loose end, so I thought I would come and see your mother,' she lied bravely, and his eyes narrowed.

'No, that's not good enough,' he said. 'Come on, back inside both of you. I want to know what's going on behind my back.'

Then a thought seemed to strike him.

'Elizabeth! It isn't Elizabeth, is it? She's all right, isn't she?'

Mrs Duncan looked at her son, then her eyes met Catherine's, almost painfully.

'No, it isn't Elizabeth, darling. Well, it is, in a way. Miss Lyall came to tell me something, and . . . well, I rather think I have to talk to you, Mike.'

About the Sheridans.'

'Oh,' he said grimly. 'Well, if that's all, I don't want to hear. No doubt they have brainwashed Catherine, too.'

'You're the one who has been brainwashed, dear,' said his mother sadly. 'You've brainwashed yourself, helped by me. I've let you think for years that your father was . . . well, some sort of saint. But if it hadn't been for James Sheridan, he would probably have ended up in jail.'

'I'll go,' said Catherine hurriedly, after a quick glance at Michael's face. It was better to leave Mrs Duncan and Michael to work this out for themselves.

'Oh no, you don't,' said Michael, gripping her arm. 'You're involved in this, and I want to know what's been going on behind my back, and why you came at all.'

'I came because of Elizabeth,' she told him flatly. 'She's been very ill. She had an accident and fell downstairs, but she's getting better now,' she assured him. 'I came for her sake. I . . . I think she needs you, Michael.'

'She has nothing but contempt for me.'

'As you had for her . . . or her family. It's all wrong, Michael. I want your mother to tell you why it's wrong, then I want you to tell Elizabeth.'

'You certainly don't believe in interfering!'
Again she flushed.

'I suppose I deserve that, but . . .'

'But you ought to be thanking her,' broke in Mrs

Duncan, 'and so should I. It's time you knew the real truth, Michael, so sit down and listen.'

It was quite late when Catherine insisted that she really must go home. It had been an upsetting evening, and when Mr Duncan had arrived home, and poked his head round the door to find his wife talking earnestly to her son, he looked vaguely surprised, and withdrew a little.

'Wait a moment, George dear,' she called. 'This is Catherine Lyall, who used to work with Michael. Catherine, I wonder if I could ask you to do something for me? Could you help George to make some tea? I really must finish telling Michael.'

'Of course,' said Catherine, rising quickly.

In the kitchen she had glanced at George Duncan, feeling rather embarrassed, but he gave her a quick shy smile.

'I apologise that our guest should be asked to make her own tea,' he said wryly, and she grinned.

'I'm flattered. It makes me feel welcome, even if . . .' she bit her lip, 'I don't yet know whether or not it was the right thing to do.'

'If you mean that Michael is now learning rather more about his father, whom I knew very well, then I'm sure he . . . and I . . . will have cause to thank you.'

It shook Michael rather badly. At first he argued furiously with his mother, then it was obvious that his own memory was stirring, of days when there wasn't enough to eat, and his shoes had to wait before being mended.

'It wasn't his fault,' Joan insisted. 'There was nothing which could help him. Nowadays people understand these social problems much better, and can do something, but not then.'

'But it's been a lie,' said Michael. 'All this time I've been living a lie! I've sweated and stewed, and I've hated the Sheridans because I thought it was their fault.'

'Elizabeth, too?' asked Catherine softly.

'I told you before,' he said roughly, 'she hates me. She hates me for extending things to John. I was rotten to them . . . even if it had been all true. I can see now that it was all wrong. It's something I'll have to live with.'

'Don't blame yourself too much, darling. You didn't know.'

He laughed shortly. 'No, I didn't, did I?' Then he turned to Catherine. 'I'll take you home in my car. It's lucky I was out on deliveries tonight. Quite often I walk. It saves money.'

She wanted to ask if his new business was prospering, but felt that she had interfered enough. Already she was very conscious of the anger in him, and meekly accepted the lift home.

'Then . . . aren't you going to see Elizabeth?' she asked, as they stopped outside the gates of Balgower. That, after all, was why she had gone to see

Mrs Duncan in the first place.

'What for? Do you really think Elizabeth will want anything to do with me now?'

'Yes, I do. I think she still loves you, Michael.'

'How young you are, Catherine!'

She flushed and opened the car door.

'I can see I've wasted my time.'

He caught her hand as she started to get out.

'No. I had to know. I'm glad to know. Later . . . well, I might stop being bitter, but it's better for the truth to come out. I . . . I shall write and apologise to James Sheridan, and to John, and perhaps to Elizabeth, though I shan't expect a reply. Goodnight, Catherine. Perhaps you ought to try for John, after all!'

He drove away as a tall figure walked towards the gate, and Catherine's heart leapt as she recognised John. He stared after Michael's car, and she stood where she was, waiting for him to walk up to her.

'I trust you've had a pleasant evening,' he said icily.

'Not exactly,' she said, 'but I don't regret it. I think a lot of misunderstanding has been cleared up.'

'Congratulations!'

She wanted to explain to him about Michael, but hardly knew where to start. In any case, John was in a rage, as she could see when they entered the hall, and was obviously in no mood to listen.

'It was a misunderstanding, John,' she insisted quietly.

'Well, spare me the details tonight,' he told her.
'I'm going to bed. Goodnight, Catherine.'

'Goodnight,' she whispered.

It seemed as though she would never get a goodnight kiss!

John's black mood was only kept under control by
firm discipline the following day, and towards six
o'clock he came over and told Catherine that he
would be ready, shortly, to drive her home, after he
had helped his father to lock up. Mr Sheridan was
going to a meeting, and wouldn't be coming with
them.

It was only after John had turned left, when he
normally turned right, that Catherine realised they
weren't, in fact, going home.

'Where are you taking me?' she asked.

'Where we can talk,' he told her briefly,
'sensibly, I hope. Then we'd better have some
food. I'm starving, if you aren't.'

She had been, but now her appetite was slipping
away as nerves gripped her stomach, but she got
out of the car obediently as John led her into a small,
quiet restaurant. He took Catherine's coat as well
as his own, and hung them near the door, then he
came back to sit down opposite her, and stare at her
across the table.

'I've had a hell of a day,' he acknowledged. 'I
don't want another like it. I've been angry, and
jealous, and I've wanted to come over and shake you

at times. I thought I knew you, Catherine, but sometimes I don't know you at all. Do you really love Mike Rodgers?'

' No,' she said firmly. ' He still loves Elizabeth.'

' He's got a funny way of showing it.'

' It wasn't his fault. He . . . he didn't really know the true facts. He does now.'

' You went to a lot of trouble to tell him, for someone who doesn't love him.'

' For someone who loves Elizabeth,' she corrected quietly, ' though I don't expect that occurred to you, John. You only see what you want to see.'

' I've scarcely seen anything, except you, since you came,' he told her, his eyes holding hers. ' When you first came I was so afraid you would fall for Michael, and we would all be unhappy. Then I asked you to marry me, but you didn't leap at the chance. I love you, Catherine. It seems to me a straightforward thing to have happened. Only you've got to go peering round corners, looking for ulterior motives, when it seems simple to me. I love you. I want to marry you. For yourself, Kate. Just you and me.'

She felt as though waves of sunshine were breaking over her head.

' What . . . what about Rosalie Craven?' she asked at last.

' There you go again! If I didn't see that smile on your face, I'd just about give up. Just about! Rosalie and I knew exactly where we stood with one another when she gave me back my ring. I wasn't grateful at the time. I was later . . . as soon as you walked in with Dad. I prayed then that you would never go away, Catherine. Please answer me properly this time. Yes or no?'

'Yes.'

'Then hurry up and eat the rest of this food, then we can go home and start living again.'

But it was some time before they arrived home, and by then Catherine's cheeks were scarlet, and her lips warm with being kissed.

'Could I ask you something, darling?' she said at length. 'Could my pearl be made into an engagement ring?'

He frowned thoughtfully.

'Wouldn't you prefer diamonds and we could have the pearl put into a pendant?'

She shook her head.

'I think it would be the wonderful link I need between you and . . . and my old home.'

'You could sell it for lots of money, probably.'

'Do you want me to have lots of money?'

John glowered.

'You need spanking for that.' He kissed her instead. 'The firm has been going through poor times, but every week brings improvement, so I'll have something decent to offer you.'

'Now you need the set-down,' she told him. 'What about the pearl, though?'

' I don't see why not, if it's really what you want.'

' It is,' said Catherine. ' Come on, let's tell Aunt Lucille and Uncle James. And Elizabeth. Will they be pleased, do you think?'

' What do you think?' asked John. ' They've been pushing me into it for weeks!'

His eyes glinted again with laughter, but she had learned to laugh with him.

' And if Michael writes to Elizabeth, and she decides to reply . . . you'll welcome him back again, for her sake, won't you, John? I know Uncle James and Aunt Lucille will, when he explains properly. They're the kind of people who don't bear grudges.'

' And I am?'

Again she was learning.

' No, darling . . . sorry. Only it will be nice to see Elizabeth happy, too.'

He grinned.

' I'll give him two days, then I'll go and bring him here by the hair of the head. Will that do?'

' That will do fine.'

Together they went, arm in arm, to tell the family.

Why the smile?

... because she has just received her **Free Harlequin Romance Catalogue!**

... and now she has a complete listing of the many, many Harlequin Romances still available.

... and now she can pick out titles by her favorite authors or fill in missing numbers for her library.

You too may have a **Free Harlequin Romance Catalogue** (and a smile!), simply by mailing in the coupon below.